Aimless Writings

by
James Dye

authorHOUSE®

AuthorHouse™
1663 Liberty Drive, Suite 200
Bloomington, IN 47403
www.authorhouse.com
Phone: 1-800-839-8640

First published by AuthorHouse 11/27/2007

ISBN: 978-1-4343-4434-2 (sc)

Printed in the United States of America
Bloomington, Indiana

This book is printed on acid-free paper.

Photo by Jeremy Zinnel

Layout design by James Dye

Website www.myspace.com/jamesdyewritings

Introduction to Aimless Writings

Bold, Beautiful, and thought provoking. From beginning to end, *Aimless Writings* will make you think. I have spent countless hours putting together a collection of writings to incite, provoke, and inspire. Every page is a journey to the very depth of my soul as I question the world around me and fight the war inside of myself. Some of the issues that I talk about aren't the most popular and may somewhat be offensive. Although I may be a little outspoken, I am a Christian and an artist. I spent several years writing, advancing my skills as a musician, and being the vocalist (and front man) of a Christian hardcore rock band known as SakeRed. The band may have been a small achievement to some but it was the whole world to me. I'll forever be in debt to the blessings I received from being in that band and this book is a result of that. I think every dream deserves to be chased no matter how inconceivable and unrealistic it may be. We all will live this life once and there's no reason to have barriers in front of the things we want the most. There are writers out there that believe that they need to go through a four year degree before they're worthy enough to write a book but I wasn't about to let that stop me.

I hope that what I write can somehow help someone and impact them in a way that will cause them to put their creativity to good use. Unity is an amazing feeling and writing this book has helped me quite a bit in that regard. It's made me closer to God and more aware of who I really am and what I stand for. My writings will confront several issues including love, death, and other personal vices. I put common emotions and scenarios into my writings including the darker ones. I have also included many unique stories filled with humor. I am a guy who likes to laugh and for some crazy reason, the most off the wall things have happened to me. I'm not a walking body full of hurtful emotions with the absence of laughter. There will be plenty of serious emotions and entertainment. This book is also meant to reflect the human mind and the thoughts we have. The things on our minds are always changing and aren't always planned. We as humans have random thoughts and dreams.

In *Aimless Writings*, I try to capture that process so that one will feel like they're reading someone else's mind, and life, in a book. It is my hope that you will read this and somehow be able to relate, and to somehow be changed. If you're not changed by my book, I hope I at least succeeded in giving you something to laugh at. You've made it this far...

I Was Saved

Years ago, I went to a youth group all-nighter and had a night that I'll never forget. At that time I was attending Moeller Road Wesleyan Church and going to the weekly youth group they had. The night started off with a treasure hunt. We had to take pictures at certain landmarks and do certain things to get points. After the treasure hunt, we went and played laser tag at Lazer X here in Fort Wayne. Then after that, we stopped at a church on Spring Street to listen to praise and worship, and to listen to a guest speaker. I had no idea that this would be one of the biggest nights of my entire life. For one of the first times, I felt the true nature of praise and worship. I sang along to every song and I listened to every single word. The energy really built up in the sanctuary after a few songs. I felt my heart racing and my eyes began to water. After the music was over, it was time for our guest speaker. I don't remember what the message was about because it was a really long time ago, but I will never forget what happened. We had a long prayer time and he was going around praying with a lot of kids and speaking with them. After a night of beautiful music and an amazing message, I was finally ready to cry. Some will say that the music and heartfelt speaking was nothing more than a tool to provoke sensitive feelings, but that's not true. God was a big influence on that entire night. God was walking with us during the treasure hunt, at laser tag, and while singing praise and worship, but was also speaking through an ordinary man who had an extraordinary experience.

After I saw our speaker walking around talking to the other kids, I felt that I had to say something to him as well. I didn't know what to say or why I felt like I had to say anything at all. Deep down I knew that I had to approach him no matter what. So I'm making my way to this ordinary man and my heart is heavy with all sorts of emotion. I'm dead in front of him and I began to weep. I had to tell him that his message had made an impact on me but I couldn't speak. The only thing I could do was cry. He held onto me for a few minutes and said something similar to, "I know…I know…and God knows too. He'll never let you go." I spent a good portion of my life letting all sorts of negative things build up, and this entire night was meant for me to let go. I was rescued by a man that I never spoke to, because he already had all the words. I've had a hard life and many unforgettable experiences. God used this night to speak to me and plant a seed. The youth pastor asked everyone, who knelt at the altar, to stay afterwards to speak about what was on our hearts. One by one, we all stood and spoke exactly what was on our hearts. I felt that there was something that God really wanted me to do, but I had no idea how to do it. So when it was my turn, I told everyone that I wanted to start a Christian band and help people the same way that I was helped by my favorite Christian bands. I told everyone that I didn't know where to start or what to do, and my friend Joey stood up behind me. He placed his hand on my shoulder and said, "I'll start this band with you bro." I had no idea that this night was going to be the foundation for one of the biggest ventures of my life. I closed the night by playing a song on the piano for all of those who stayed behind. We all exchanged hugs, and ended an amazing night with love.

A few months prior to the youth group "all-nighter," I had started my initial transition to Christian music. I went through severe depression and even contemplated suicide. My early teenage years were so filled with confusion that I didn't know what to do. I was listening to the most depressing music that you could imagine. One night, I went to my favorite laser tag venue (the same one I went to at the "all-nighter") and I talked to some of my friends that worked there. I heard this band playing on the speakers in the arcade and the music really drew me in. I asked them what band was playing and they told me Project 86. Naturally, I wanted to know more about this band. My friend gave me a burned copy of their first CD. I immediately put it in my CD player and all the horrible things I was feeling began to turn into fuel. I listened to that copy so many times that it wouldn't play in the CD player anymore. Instead of hurting myself and dwelling in my depression, I was building immunity from the hurtful things I was enduring. This was a humongous turn in my life. I went to a Christian bookstore called; "The Anchor Room" and I bought any CD that interested me.

I became addicted to these bands, and their message, because of the transformation I had experienced. I made countless trips to that bookstore to buy any CD I could get my hands on. I definitely give those bands credit for making me into the man that I am today. I saw how powerful music could be first hand. Some people don't understand my fascination with my favorite bands, but they also don't know what their music helped me through and what it continues to do for me. My early teenage years were the foundation I needed for starting up my own band, and the youth group all-nighter was the confirmation of that mission.

Breathe Forever Tonight

The air is getting harder to breathe

We could drive our fists in the ground forever

What would make a man turn a gun on himself?

It's just a dream to think there's a good night's sleep

To think every thought led up to this moment

The air is getting harder to breath

We could pray until our hearts burn forever

What would make someone say they never loved me?

It's just a dream to think every story ends happy

To think that there's actually pain in this world

Approaching paper with another pen in hand

I'm tattooing this piece of tree with my ink

To persuade everyone that there's something else inside of me

That's casually seen

Make things right before you die

Silence is golden and the biggest cause of death in me

I'm tattooing this piece of tree with my ink

To persuade everyone that there's something else inside of me

In memory of Travis

It's Illegal to Break a Foundation

Never again will the nails be driven into the foundation, the
foundation of love
Never again will silence represent us, maintain and secure the
foundation
The foundation of love
Steadfast, hold your ground
We are not dead
We are not alone
We die for the foundation
Another nail in your hand and in mine
Another day is dead and gone

Here After

All I ever needed from you was one final goodbye
All I ever needed to do was mend these wings and fly
Blessed be the broken, we are the strongest of heart
I was nothing more than a love
And I was just aimlessly walking your way
But the fire is still burning
The fire is still burning under my skin
The message isn't stopping
Until we've reached the end

The Best of Both Worlds

Walk in the path of trials
Here in this moment and I don't feel anything
I am so full of this hollow world but I'm okay
I smile through the tears and I live through death
Now I count the years
Now salvation is all that I've got left
Loss of control
Lack of control
I will prevail
I will prevail
Because I have a soul
Walk in the path of love
Here in this still life and I do not feel the change
I am fixed in this broken world but its okay
I still stand
I scream through the silence
And I will not silence my message
I climb out of these ashes and now it's my time to rise
I will prevail
Where my heart is bound
I won't make a sound
I will prevail

Never Insult a Karaoke Singer

My junior year of high school was filled with all sorts of excitement because, in general, I am an exciting guy. I always thought that school dances were kind of lame but I always enjoyed going to them anyways. The dances seem to always consist of trashy rap music and one hit wonder rock hits. I tried to be as ravishing as possible when it was time to slow dance. I would usually ask my dream girl to slow dance with me, but that was only when I wasn't dating someone. There was a weird incident that occurred during one of the dances and that was karaoke. The disk jockey chose at least three people to come on stage and sing. The only songs I remember were, "Pretty Fly for a White Guy," and "With Arms Wide Open." The first song sounded goofy enough and I didn't feel that they should continue this embarrassing display of bad singing voices. I didn't happen to see who was up there singing and I wasn't sure I wanted to. I can sing decent, although I'm surely not the best at it. I just didn't think those were the best songs to have someone sing karaoke. I remembered the second song sounding absolutely awful but there was nothing I could do about it.

The next day, all the students in my art class talked about the dance and how it was different having a few people do karaoke. We had to sketch portraits of our art partners and overall everyone seemed to think that the karaoke singing was pretty cool but they didn't seem to like the first couple songs. I immediately jumped in the conversation and began to tell my opinions of the dance. I began to tell them how I didn't think any of the singers were very good and it was like hearing the sound of nails being scratched down a chalkboard. I proceeded to tell them that I thought the guy that did the worst was the one who sang, "With Arms Wide Open." Strangely enough, the class grew so quiet that one could hear a pin drop to the floor. I was starting to think highly of myself because I had the whole class's attention. After awhile, I realized how mean I was starting to sound and I truly didn't mean it to come out that way. I told everyone that I had never heard anyone who sang that song as badly as him and that I couldn't believe they even let him on stage. Not only was the class extremely quiet, but they also had their mouths dropped in shock. I began to look around at all of them and I simply asked, "What?" Right afterward I had finally realized what created such shocking reactions from my class mates.

My art partner, whom was sitting directly in front of me, said, "James, that was me." I totally felt like a big jerk. My stomach felt like it was tied in a knot and I sank low in my chair as if I could hide and no one would notice. When I peeked over my desk, everyone still looked shocked and so did my art partner. I didn't feel like an apology would help whatsoever but I tried anyways. I said, "I'm so sorry dude. I feel like the biggest jerk in the world and had no right to say that." He pointed inward to his heart and said, "James that hurt...right here." I felt even worse than before. I started to feel a little better though because he started laughing. He thought it was funny that I bashed him so much, only for me to find out that I was talking about him. He shrugged it off and told me that everything was cool and that there weren't any hard feelings. Never, under any circumstances, insult a karaoke singer because they could possibly be your friend.

I Call You Father

I will always fail you and I will never be perfect like you. What I will do, is love you. I will love you and have faith in your words. I'll never forget that it is you, and you alone, that created my heart. You instilled the greatest gift that was ever in existence. You gave me love. My beating heart was created by you and the breaking of my heart is mended by you. In times of joy, and times of tragedy, I will remember what you've done for me. There are many out there that see you the way I do, and there are many who don't. You are forever. Some say that you're nothing more than a historic person. Some say that you're not real. I've witnessed to people that don't have a single good thought about your name.

I call you Redeemer, I call you the Mender of Hearts, and I call you Father.

Time

It seems I'm always searching for something to blame
The clock keeps on ticking though I've never felt the same
Minute after minute
Hour after hour
I can't talk about God without people wanting my soul devoured
I am one among the many who bleed
A hand in forgiveness is all you'll ever need
I will be the one to burn this cage and free my soul from this
plagued rage
Time has been a scar
It always drags us down when we get so far
Time has plagued my face
It showed no remorse in my disgrace
I will start the revolution
I will never fade
Time brings pain just the same way every day
So I step inside to change my life
Survive this world and take away the strife
I know how to live
This soul is something my God has given

Not Every Rainbow Is Perfect

You become my mission and my desire
When all of my questions have been answered
And the words burn into my heart
For a moment I shared stories with you
Beginnings to remember and endings to die for
The planets aligned for the spark in our eyes
And the beauty of our conversation
I pray for what's happening inside of me
The new life that bestows the greatest glow
I want to be more than enough
My attention is bought
Because everything I read is a promise
Sometimes things are meant to be
Within the signs of sidewalk chalk
Let's believe
A line is the distance between two points
And the distance between me and you
We become the vastness behind everything
I never knew I'd be bleeding on the fire escape
And I'm doing everything to erase my sleeve
I relocated my heart and put it where it goes
My heart rate speeds up at the sight of you
As we sketch solace with the precision of a surgeon
We picture ourselves in different frames
Because tonight we lay the stars to sleep

Partners in Crime

It's your time and my dime
We know exactly where we're going
No matter what they say
I've got the ignition
And the vault is only a heartbeat away
You've got the entrance covered
My number one scout
The getaway car and always looking out
There's no need for guns on our run
We're together in the chasing
Friends to the end
A bullet of its own casing
Whether it be a time of crisis or bad day
You'd stitch me up
And send me on my way
If you fell, you know I'd catch you
I'd stand you to your feet
And I'd admire the view of friendship
Pedal to the metal
We've got places to go unseen
I thank you for my share of the earnings
Your friendship means everything
If there was a challenge
We'll rise against the things we're facing
Because we're together in the chasing
Friends to the end
A bullet of its own casing
We know exactly where we're going
No matter what they say
Partners in crime
It's your time and my dime

The Hardest Decision

I wish I may, I wish I might
Be told the truth from my heart tonight
I'm holding on to the most distant hope
As I slide and die
On the most slippery slope
To say what I feel with accurate precision
Do I listen to my heart or my mind?
That can be the deadliest, yet hardest decision

A Tribute

I just don't really know if you'll be leaving when they say you will be
The things to come may be my greatest disease
But you taught me music, the kind that puts the heart to ease
Whether it's today, tomorrow, or a year from now
Your love is forever embodied in my piano's keys
I owe every ounce of that talent to God
Because he used you to plant the seed
That very essence is in me....from every show,
Every lyric, every hand shake, and every scream
You taught me music....
The greatest escape of my life

Cancer Is More Than a Constellation

I am a disease of viral intentions
You'll never know when I'll take over
I'll make you second guess your life
I'll make you thankful for what you have
Your time is shortened completely
And you'll feel so far away from recovery
I become more than a disease
I become a matter of the heart and soul
You'll reevaluate your life by letting God
And certainly letting go
He'll listen to you more than you'll ever know
In closing I will say
I have no preference of the type of person you are
What race or even age
I consume good and bad people
And I change the perspective of each and every day

Fast Food Horror Stories

Driving to Taco Bell on the way home from shows became a tradition. My car was pulled up by the speaker and I was getting ready to order. The fast food worker said, "Welcome to Taco Bell what can I get for you?" I calmly replied, "Just a minute please." Then I got the standard, "Take all the time you need, order when you're ready." By this time my band mates had pulled up behind me honking and yelling. Somehow the worker heard the yelling and came to the conclusion that it was me. She got really angry with me. She said, "I told you to order when you're ready!" She continued to be extremely rude to me when I started ordering. I told her that I wanted a cheesy gordita crunch and she answered, "We don't have that!" I asked, "Since when?" and she replied, "Since forever because we've never had them." That was shocking to me because every Taco Bell in existence had them. I yelled back, "Fine! I don't want one then." We pulled to the window and she practically threw the bags at me, with the sauce, and I got grumpier than I was before. All this hostility came from my band mates yelling at me in the drive through.

It seems like all my fast food problems occurred at a Taco Bell. There was a time that I stopped at a Taco Bell/KFC and I was slightly rear ended in the drive through. I looked in my rear view mirror and saw an older couple that must have been double dating with their friends. I was in a good mood and I wasn't going to cause any trouble over it. They were all laughing hysterically. I was in a good mood so I started laughing as well. Every time that we stopped at a Taco Bell, on the way to a show, I would get a bunch of girlie looking temporary tattoos and I would go into the bathroom and apply them to make my band mates laugh. I would also get a huge laugh out of changing my voice in the drive through. Sometimes I was Canadian, red neck, or overly sensitive and cheerful. There was another fast food nightmare when some friends and I were on the way back from a Project 86 concert. Naturally the incident occurred at the local Taco Bell. Their speaker was damaged and the lady couldn't hear one word I said. I kept telling her that it was broken but she didn't understand. So I start rattling off our order and correcting her every few minutes. I repeated the phrase "soft tacos" at least a hundred times. "So you want two hard tacos?" I replied, "No! I want two soft tacos!" "Okay sir, it sounds like you want two hard tacos?" Then I kept repeating that same phrase over and over. Finally, I give up and drive to the first window. I went over the whole order with the cashier and told him the speaker was broken. He asked me, "Did you say you wanted two hard tacos?" I just laughed and told him soft tacos. He gave us a sweet hook up for all our troubles.

There probably isn't any food out there scarier than gas station sandwiches. My friend Adam and I would get really brave and try out different ones. Surprisingly, they're not all that bad depending on the gas station and what kind of sandwich you get. Stay away from soy jalapeño cheese burgers. They give you heart burn and cause you to breath fire on small villages. I also remember my friend Adam and I being stuck in a drive through line at McDonalds for a little over a half an hour. We were stuck between vehicles and paid already so there was no turning back. I ordered a filet o' fish and I was disappointed. It was a smashed thing hardly worthy of being called a sandwich. I poked the bun and a perfect hole was made by my finger yet I don't remember asking it to be toasted. I ate it anyways because I was starving and it wasn't too bad. The most outrageous McDonald's incident happened when I went to pick up lunch for my coworkers. I went through everyone else's order and then I finally got to mine. This incident also involved a filet o' fish.

I politely told the lady I wanted a filet o' fish and she looked at me the same way a deer gazes into a pair of headlights. Then she replied, "You want a McFlurry?" I calmly said, "No, just a filet o' fish." She looked confused again and the next thing she said was beyond my understanding. I don't think one person in this entire world would understand this crazy response. She said, "Chocolate and bananas?" I freaked out. Never in a million years have I witnessed such a confusing answer. I tried so hard to keep my emotions at bay and it was just no use. I angrily answered, "No! I want a fish sandwich!" This employee said another thing that shocked me for some reason.

She said, "Why didn't you just say so?" I find it hard to believe that she'd catch on to the phrase "fish sandwich" compared to her marvelous answer of chocolate and bananas. The majority of my fast food encounters occurred on the road trips I'd take with my band and when I car-pooled my friends to the shows. So beware of what food you eat and where you eat it from.

Disclaimer: These are personal stories of the author and the places that these incidents occurred at. The dialog is fictitious and loosely based the real conversations and does not reflect the views, employees, or service of these restaurants.

Ps- My band and I stopped at a rest stop to fill up on snacks and there was a crazy guy on a motorcycle. He decided to be a show-off and popped a wheelie. He fell off the back of his motorcycle and the bike kept going without him. His muffler, and other parts, were scattered all over the parking lot.

A Clenched Fist

I always wondered why you held me tight
Blew a kiss and pushed in the knife
Ran me over and ran me through
Before there was emptiness
There was you...
But who we were isn't who we are
We fell too short and came so far
Just characters posing for pictures
Just actors in a wardrobe of stitches
No one knows just what's at stake
Why do we fix things that break?
Just grab the glue...it will make it okay
Maybe I'm stronger than what you say
I must confess

I Think I Liked You Better When You Didn't Know Me

The days are numbered and I'm falling under
I know that this world is fading, but I'll never fade
I know now, that I will rise again
Can you fix me?
Can you save me?
I feel like I'm the only one
Who's caught in this game?
In this cutting circle I'm bound and broken
I feel so dead and so broken
It's so easy to see God
But it's hard to see the enemy
Was it the beginning of you, or the end of me?
I think I liked you better when you didn't know me
And my heart wasn't encased in glass
In this broken shell I know only time will tell
It reminds me of days when I longed for separation
I think I liked you better when I knew myself
With hope as a shield and faith as a weapon
I think I liked you better when you didn't know me
And my heart wasn't broken
Somebody hold me while the old me
Starts to die and I'm dying out
Can you fix me?
Can you save me?

Roadside Construction

I can't help but wonder if you'd just walk by with an unfamiliar look in your eye as I lay dead by the roadside. Maybe you wouldn't lend a hand if I was falling in quicksand because now a day, abandonment is such a high demand. Maybe I'm wrong and you've cared all along, it's just forever is a long time to say you'll be gone. I tried to make my words few because your words hurt too. What ends this madness? I wish I knew, because nothing I did, done, or could do…would ever explain why you said, "I don't care about you." Rest assured knowing that it would catch my eye if you were lying dead by the roadside, because I'm the kind of guy that won't just walk by.

With warmest regards,

Me, the Samaritan

An Angry Text Message

I have been measured and weighed
Labeled with a price tag much to my dismay
Complying with standards that I shouldn't hold
Allowing myself to be burned at the stake
By your misguided barcode
I'm in the process of mending my heart
An endeavor to heal what fell apart
I can't say your time is well spent
Pretending that my impact didn't make a dent
I was beauty, I was love
I was the greatest gift from above
A priceless gift bartered at a pawn shop
The simple thought of being less to you
Than I was, is enough to make my heart stop
There are no intentions of good faith and amends
I'm important to God, and unlike you,
His love never ends.

I Would Name Her Rock and Roll

The letters of her name are another spelling for love.
She defines it so well.
A beauty, a love, and a blessing
Her movement is much like a dance
My heart plays music that she would listen to
There aren't any blades
There aren't any ghosts
No journals to reference this breeze
Wind abrasion is the common torture
She is the wind
Our lives intertwine beyond reasoning
Music is always a common factor
It can add and subtract, make or break
It can personify this beauty
When beauty is personified
Music is my love and my passion
It's a melody that I can connect with metaphors
So when I say, "her" or "she"
It's a substitution for music
She has a style I can relate with
A constant thought when I fall
If her style had a name
I would name her rock and roll

You Spoke, I Listened

I spoke with torment today and it twisted my arm a bit
It gave me a run for my money and took me for everything I had
It took me for a ride and walked a mile with me
Desperation leaves a mark and an imprint
There's no energy or extra force
Only submission to the most overwhelming conversations
Depression had words for me, and I had words for it
I felt as if heaven didn't recognize me
Heaven didn't know my name or my face
It turned away at the sound of my voice
I was exiled and banished from the gates
My identification card wouldn't swipe me in
And the maintenance man was on break
Why must I be here and face this?
Have I been an evil person that God does not recognize?
I know this isn't so, but I still have to wonder
It's easy to look for Him in times of struggle
But even harder in times of perfection
I wrote everything off and settled for the gallows
I stumbled, fell, and choked
And when I doubted the most...
That's when heaven spoke
I wasn't too drunk with sorrow to notice
I questioned if I knew the voice or the language
But I wasn't so far into myself that I couldn't see
And I was all the more grateful
When heaven spoke to me

Lay To Waste, Oh Fiery Furnace

Temptation is the mark of a dead man
I hope I'm not a dead man inside
When I'm thrown in, I pray I won't burn
Because I know the meaning of a promise
As I stand firm and steadfast
There is a storm coming
And there's a ghost that's calling me
Sound the anthem it's stronger than a gun
Rise from the ashes, we are the chosen ones
Bring out the looking glass
There's more than our eyes can see
Love will always prevail over evil
And that I do believe
So say good bye to the turning tide
That's spread across the shore
Lay to waste, oh fiery furnace
I fear your flame no more

Attack of the Panics

I can't control these inner demons
That seeks to destroy
The ones keep me from living
And make me want to die
Let me go and leave me alone
I don't want you and I want to go home
Let me breathe and let me believe
That someday I'll be without you
Longing for the end of this imbalance
I want to breathe comfortably
I want to love like there's no tomorrow
A quick change of pace to replace this sorrow
I'm half of who I am when you're with me
And you're never unseen
Sometimes it seems like a pipedream
To drive down the road of recovery
And place you on a shelf
You keep breaking my heart
And making me less of myself
I'm waiting for the day
When I feel alive and end with embrace

Carlie

One day we all will learn to fly
Be made complete in heaven's eye
Someday we'll never fear to live
One day we'll never fear to die
But I died today
When I saw your face
Ignite the fire that burns in me
So I can live through you

You and I, we dance in tragedy
Amidst a nightfall that took everything away from us
What could we do?
I know the stars shine brighter for you
Now I'm left here all alone with nothing
But my memories to sustain me
I want to know why
I died today when I saw your face

Everything that binds me is left
I'm left here with these memories of you
I'll never forget what I saw on the TV screen
I want to know why I died today
When I saw your face

In memory of Carlie

Caution Tape

Sometimes it's so easy to tear down the caution tape
When it covers your mouth
And when there's still a thorn in your side
I'd prefer stitches over dissolvable lace any day
Because we know what makes it better
A dose as misguided as a missile
An instrument of violence to the highest degree
Perhaps nothing struck my face so hard
At the end of the day and after everything you say
There's still me standing in the door way
A constant reminder of where you've been
And what you did
You hurt yourself by hurting me
And now your reign is at its end

A Concrete Landscape

More anguish, I have found
Keep sakes that linger in the shadows
And make me unaware of their existence
They tie a knot into my heartstrings
And I'm rendered helplessly to the floor
I used to call it treasure
It's of no worth now or ever
I'm afraid I won't understand
I'm submissive to the ailments of my own walk
I can't be sure if I'll know love's name
Or know love's face
Until I'm sitting beside God
And the hollowness is replaced

Dance with Me

I'd compliment you with a kiss if I could
Nothing can really predict the outcome
I thought about you when I saw that shooting star
My first reaction is my hand upon your face
You have an inward beauty that seems to radiate
And maybe I'm just hanging by a rope
I can't think about anything else right now
I don't know why and I don't know what to do
Because I don't want to face the truth
That my emotions commit suicide over and over
If I could, I'd take solace in you
I'd take a chance and ask you to dance
In this new awakening
My whole life has painted the sky
And I'm embraced with glass
As I walk with you in my mind
I could lie beneath the stars
And look up to perfect clarity
I hope the thought in the back of your mind
Could possibly be me
Somehow I can't give up and I believe
I would take a chance and ask you to dance
In this dream that I've been dreaming

Scripted Lines

I guess I should thank you for my inspiration
My words are like the sand in the hour glass
They are many and sift over the course of time
A dismal day in February
Is like the coldest day in December
A month I'll never forget
A broken promise that I'll always remember
You can hear my voice
My love, you can see
A hand you can feel
Followed by text you can read
A story of perseverance,
And reasons to believe
Now I'll let you read a narrative,
These scripted lines of me

Midnight Flashback

For a short time I was happy too
Everything was going my way
And all things were new
The sky was the color I painted it
And I was loved by you
The sun was just the way I liked it
And the cool winds blew
Like a volcano, my heart was ready to erupt
The sky was no longer my color
Because I was starting to wake up
What I wouldn't give
To sleep a little longer

Tonight, I Trust No One

Tonight I feel a little cold
I am a pretty brave person but sometimes I'm not
Sometimes my exterior is the stronghold
And everything inside is paralyzing when destroyed
I don't understand why I feel guilty for helping myself
Sometimes I think chivalry is dead
And I constantly wonder the true intentions of a good deed
We all must be wearing masks and drinking from flasks
I trust no one
My trust has been betrayed
It's like the weight of a gun is upon my heart
I realize that there's no such thing as perfection
I can only hope
My hope has been betrayed
Tonight I feel a little remorseful for things I didn't do
I am pretty strong but sometimes I'm not
Sometimes I build bridges and sometimes I tear them down
And everything inside is paralyzing when destroyed
I don't understand why I feel guilty for writing
Sometimes I think my words are dead
And I constantly wonder if my writings can change anything
We all must write in order to sleep better at night
I only trust God

Paris in the Spring

My heart still skips a beat
Due to my abandonment
Wondering what's left for me
Just as a tree's branches bleed the sky
I say see you later, never good bye
A doused and rekindled fire ironic as it seems
Is the lifespan of our hearts?
Over shadowed by our dreams
My heart still skips a beat
And due to my abandonment, I wonder what's left of me
Just as a tree's branches bleed the sky
The finite line of see you later
The infinite path of good bye

A Phone Call That I'll Never Forget

A long time ago, I received a mysterious phone call. The call was made around 3:30am and I was asleep. My mom happened to be sleeping in the living room that night and she got up to answer the phone. My mom said, "Hello?" and the voice answered, "Let me talk to James right now." Then she replied, "I'm not waking him up at 3:30 in the morning." The voice repeatedly demanded my mom to wake me up for the phone call and my mom wouldn't give him an inch. They argued for another minute or two and then the stranger said something that I'll never forget. The guy was silent for a moment and he was getting ready to say his final line. He said, "I have a message for James. Tell him there is no God." My mom was extremely scared of that phone call. The next morning she wakes me and tells me about this crazy phone call that I received at 3 in the morning. At first I thought she was joking because sometimes she talks in her sleep. I said, "Are you sure you weren't just dreaming or something?" She replied, "James check the caller ID and tell me what you see."

I cycled through the caller I.D. to prove to my mom that she was just sleeping. Sure enough there were two phone calls at the exact same time that she told me. To this very day, I don't know who that person was or why he had to deliver that message. He must have been someone poor in spirit and hurting a great deal. The scary thing is he knew my name so he had to have known me somehow. I just wonder what made him do that. I often wondered if he was in a lot of emotional pain and was angry at God. I may never solve the mystery of who he was, but I periodically pray for him. He obviously needed it. I hope there will be a day when he'll seek me out and confess. I don't want an apology or anything like that. I just want to know who he is and ask him if he's okay. That was definitely a phone call that I'll never forget.

Carry Me

So far from what I used to be inside
Now I feel so lost and now I feel cold
Carry me inside with love
I have gone away from you
Now I can go on, with you
From life, in time
I love the way you are
That you'd forgive me this far
Now I'm torn in two
Because I lived a life without
You are my God
Now it's time to part
The old life that I once lived
Carry me inside with love
I have gone away from you
Now I can go on with you
From life this time
I loved the way you carried me

Crossing Paths with a Killer

God save us from this darkness we've become
There's too much death and I can't concentrate on life
Sound off
A call to faith
There are killers in our midst
I pray for your return
I pray for your strength
Awaiting days when I feel that everything is okay
Less painful horizons
Sound off 1...2...3...
Waiting for my savior
Waiting for my solace
Waiting for my shelter
Waiting for my solace
Your love whispers like rain
Crossing paths with a killer
There's no retreat and no surrender
My heart's not silent for your silence
And I won't fall to the grave
My next door neighbor could be the killer they're looking for
There's too much death and I can't concentrate on life
Marching on and on
Like a mindless drone
We're attacked in life
We're attacked in the home
Like a bleeding dove
We yearn for the sky
Sound off 1...2...3

Fallout

No force to rise against, just two raised fists
Just two raised fists to rise again
One day I'll fall
This won't be that day
Let's go on home or take this outside
So I'm falling out and raining on your parade
Now it rains in you
It rains in me

Ghost Mode

Give me an insight on what is really seen
My rock I wield and the hand that carries it
You're not dead, but very much here
In front of me and I'm speechless
We walk these streets chasing our dreams
And then we remember how it felt being alive
Never compromising who we are
Beauty in a ghostly image
In the form of an entity in which our picture is taken
But I see beyond all of that and I see the inner beauty
That becomes you
Everything that this is
And everything that you are
The much needed release
Since the dawn of the setting sun

I Am a Ninja

I look around at random things at a red light and I notice a guy is staring at me. He starts lip syncing obscenities and I don't understand why. He starts riving up his engine like the Indy 500 is about to start. He's taunting me with his lip syncing and the engine of his car. I can't believe this guy. I don't know what it is with today's male generation. They all look like they're angry and they want to make eye contact for some unknown reason. I just don't get, but I'm ready for a fight if I need to be. There is one thing, and one thing alone that needs to be known in this situation. Obviously this guy had no idea that I'm a ninja and I'm a force to be reckoned with. I keep ninja stars holstered to my boot and a katana on my back. I bite elbows and I fight with all of my being. I lurk in the shadows and I am a restless vessel of vengeance. I am so much more than vigilant with my cat like reflexes and arsenal that would scare an army. I am a ninja. I will defeat this delinquent knave with my death stare and I will karate chop his thighs. Then I will kick his car because I, for the thousandth time, am a ninja. At least in my heart I am.

Steadfast

Prepare yourself for battle
Prepare yourself for war
You don't know what love is
Until you've had to die for it
Let's start this process over a fatality
Bestow in me a steadfast spirit
Bestow in me a steadfast heart
You want more?
I'll give you more
More to give and more
To live for

Misty Eyes

If you embrace me in doors, embrace me outside
Take me somewhere where love may reside
This serenade is hardly over because it's just begun
Lead me here or there, lead me anywhere but on
Friends and brothers alike exchange blades and hand grenades
We're too busy being temporary, and everything I reach for is
meant to fade
Oh what lies behind?
These misty eyes of mine

Like Embers

Beauty falls

I expected a "hello"

But I got a "good bye"

Staring out on a day like this

I can't help but feel content

When you say you love me...

I hear, "I'll be leaving soon."

So let's remain silent if only for a moment

And pretend that this fire will consume

Staring outside on a day like this

I can't help but feel content

s.o.s.- sorry so sloppy

w.b.s.- write back soon

bff- best friends forever

xoxo- hugs and kisses

ttyl- talk to you later

a.t.a.d.m.m.h.f.b. - All these abbreviations don't make my heart feel better.

The Heart Ache, the Embrace, and the Blade of Grass

Heart ache is as gentle as a midnight breeze
And as sharp as a blade of grass across the wrist
A ship sailing across restless seas
Broken, in the false innocence of a first kiss
Into her arms, looking away from the glare
Like increasing the voltage on an electric fence
I looked in those eyes many times, but nothing familiar there
An inescapable embrace that tightens when you resist
Memories are like a photo of a sunset
They look familiar, but we question if it was ever real
Or if it was a distortion of art
Lest, we forget
The ones that stay with you are like a stake through the heart and
as sharp as a blade of grass across the wrist....

A Complacent Replacement

When your batteries run low you can go to the store and buy replacements. But not every battery is made the same. You could wind up buying new ones and they could be an off brand or have some sort of defect. And sometimes you can only find one type of battery at a certain store. We all know that the off-brands are just a quick fix. So if you're going to throw them away make sure you know that you may not find another battery like them again. With that being said....sometimes you just need to recharge the battery that you already have because it's important in its own right. I've always believed that if you have a good thing you really shouldn't let it go regardless of the circumstances. So if you don't want that battery anymore that means that you've changed your mind about its importance, but the battery never changed.

I've been a battery before.

In Your Absence

Eternal sunshine
Eternal bliss
A frozen landscape
Shadowed by a winter kiss
Just another victim, just another face
Warm intentions are followed by a hollow embrace
Though the canvas is weak, the paint is strong
My heart is steady and I live on

Though my <3 bled, it grew to mend
I once handed you a @-----
And you looked at me as if I were an (<>..<>)
I guess you can only say good bye so many times

The Map of Endurance

Destroyed and desolate
One can always tell the change of seasons
The wind scrapes me into isolation
Tearing my heart with the greatest of ease
The map of endurance is always a hard road
We've all been wronged at some point in life
We've all been hurt by someone
Sometimes it's to the most severe degree
Its okay not to feel and it's okay to be numb
As long as you move forward
To walk in wellness is strength
To walk with wounds is bravery
And bravery can be the greatest strength
Alone and hopeful
One can always tell the turning of tides
The waves are like flames
Burning my heart with the greatest of ease
The map to forgiveness is always a hard road
We've all had a broken heart
We've all had a falling out
Sometimes it's to the most severe degree
It's okay to take your time and its okay to be numb
As long as you move forward
To walk in faith is strength
To walk wounded is strength
And wounded faith can turn into the greatest strength

Alco Hall

Swallow, drench, and diffuse
I am your enchanter and you're excuse to abuse
I make you do things that you wouldn't normally do
You're in me and I surely am in you
I am the lie that you tell
I am you're good time,
I am someone else's hell
You act like I'm in control
As if I cast some kind of spell
I destroy your kids
I influence you to destroy your relationships
I influence you to make new friends
You'll spend your money
And I'll make you mine
You'll engulf and you'll indulge
Behind me, you will hide
Make your words few
Because I am the drink
I am your reason to break things
And I am nothing
Because it's all you

Remission

I can go through my day happy and care free
But somewhere in the back of my mind
I know I could smile wider
I could laugh harder
My face could light up a little brighter
And my heart could beat a little faster
I said good bye
I wished you well
I threw away the key
I've saved myself the best that I could
Still standing, only me
In my mind, I do my best to picture you
But when you materialize...
It's a pain I don't want to relive through
You're name won't be spoken
You're pictures won't be seen
All I can think of is rising above
The things you did to hurt me
All you did was hurt yourself
And one day you will see

Digital Text vs. Inked Letters

Sometimes a heart can race
Sometimes it can skip a beat
It's when it does both,
That makes it hard to speak
In a case like that, I just won't say anything
Sometimes I sit and wonder
Sometimes it's more than it seems
It's when I wake up, that I'm scared...
That's when you're my dream
I wouldn't mind staying asleep
Some nights I just sit and write
Sometimes I think my writings would make a great display
Recently, you've been an inspiration
The pen in my hand...and the words on the page
If anything it's been a beautiful thought
And I've been thinking a lot lately

Erase Razor Blade Parade

I love the person you are
You put the beast at rest and become the night
Your words drain rivers and move mountains
I've never seen a better sight
You're not like the one with all streamers
The one that wines and dines like there's no tomorrow
She waves her hands around so carelessly
But you dance with truth and beauty
A strand that a razor blade could never cut
It just feels good to be immovable and anchored
I am myself and unshackled
Freedom rings ear to ear
Singing the loudest melodies
Erasing away all my fears
"I am new," I replied
My heart remains intact
And my dreams never die
Not like the ones who drink away and parade
I'm never defeated for very long
It's what I'm trying to say
You put the beast to rest tonight

Don't Let Go

I've tried to open locked doors
Turn me in and drown me slow
There's nothing new because I've felt this before
Not much has changed but it takes some time
I can't show the face I made so close the book
I'm not seen in the places I want to be
But I've walked so far
Only to keep my words sound proof
The status is clearly made
Implied consent when you can't say anything
Touch up paint to hide how it feels
How do I look tonight?
It's not always the simple things that chase your mind
The best part of driving is taking a ride
Returning the feeling
The more I try to fix it, the more it breaks in my hand
Whispering that I can't mend it
Lovely things that I've said
And it took so long to say it that way
Join my arms
And pull me in to heights that I can't reach

What Being a Hardcore Christian Vocalist Means To Me

The church and Jesus called all of us Christians, to be fishers of men. I wasn't always into the extreme music but I acquired a taste for it. I loved being the vocalist in a hardcore Christian band and I was very proud of it. I had to constantly defend it to other Christians of all ages. So many people write off the style just like I did at one time. What they don't understand is the passion of the lyrics in general. Hardcore music, in general, seems to have some of the most beautiful imagery and the most passionate lyrics. The stereo typical praise and worship serves a great purpose if it's your preference and it has a great purpose in the church and in the home.

What a lot of people didn't understand is that this music style was my praise and the shows were like church for me. The more I did these shows, the more people I was fortunate to meet. I became close with a lot of people that attended those shows as well as the other Christian bands that would perform. These shows felt so authentic in what I envisioned Christianity to be. There were many times I felt awkward going to church. I didn't feel like I knew whose hands I was shaking. I would shake hands with people that seemed like great men and women of God. Then outside of church, they became incredibly rude. I used to get a lot of fun poked at me for my favorite music style and what I did. I immediately became hurt and disappointed. Not only was that bashing my favorite kind of music, but it also bashed my position as a vocalist. I started to disagree with a lot of the things I saw in church. We all have views on how we think things should be and I can understand that.

The majority of the people that frowned upon my ministry never attended these shows to find out what they were about. They didn't know the passion that these shows contained. The majority of the hardcore Christian bands, that I was exposed to, poured their hearts on stage. The words were spoken with the same passion of the testimonies that are heard in church. They were never there to see how I was face first with the crowd and how they all fought for the mic during gang vocals. I'll never forget the little kids that would approach me at these shows. Most of them knew me by name and would hug me. I'll also never forget the teary eyed people that approached me to tell me what our message did for them. I wanted to look up to the sky and say, "God, have I finally done something right?" In all the evil that I am, I was able to reach others and I felt accomplished.

I hate to see anyone cry and I was lucky enough to comfort some people that cried. I think of a few people that ran away to cry and how I followed them to give them a hug. What an amazing position God put me in. I experienced things that I didn't experience behind a pew or during praise and worship. We all have our preferences and if something speaks to our hearts, we should engulf ourselves in it. So if Christian hardcore music offends, I will continue to be offensive and I will defend my claims. God said to make a joyful noise and to be fishers of men. I'm pretty sure that He is the judge of that. Please keep in mind that what I'm saying doesn't apply to all churches or Christians. I was strictly speaking about my experiences at the time. There are a lot of older adults that are getting into the style. The staff at my favorite venue consisted of parents, middle aged adults, and young adults.

The Thunder of Butterflies

You can believe me when I say
That you gave the sky a new shade of blue
There's wind in my sails and I won't turn around
I'm thinking of something beautiful to say
And when I look at you, nothing seems to hurt
Every little bit seems to be more than enough
With no distorted feelings and no poison in my blood
Magic presses from your lips onto mine
And radiates with every thing you say
I write on the walls to thank you
For inviting me in and asking me to stay
I'm looking at the skyscrapers we've created
On their own, they stand
That thunder you're hearing is the beating of my heart
And the sound of butterflies when you grab my hand

Out of Resources

I don't know when it's the right time to smile
Second guessing is all there seems to be
Hanging on the edge of a cliff
And counting reasons not to let it go
Constantly in the same place
With a steady flame and a makeshift fuse
Kissing good bye seemed to be the right thing to do
Time to let go and burn
Standing isn't what it's supposed to be
Maybe happiness is meant to be short lived
I'm not sure what I'm doing
To keep this from working
Expectations running high for what they are
I'm doomed to a sudden fate
But don't worry it's not a dent in your metal
Nor a stitch in your wound
Just the things you keep when you lock your room

Something Is Different Tonight

Hand in hand you always wonder
If it is what it seems
Waking up wondering if the night was a dream
If the shadows spread
While I fell to my sleep
It was the right time tonight
To let myself be weightless
And close my eyes
I love how you found me
With your feet off the ground
And in the middle of the street
It was the right time tonight
To be taken in
And taken by surprise
Before I had been given something new
I was looking for all the pieces
And running for glue
There was something different
Because that something was you

Love and Friendship in a Blender

I think of friendships with sort of a light heart. I've been thinking about the unforeseen outcomes that occur in life. The little curve balls that get thrown at us and they're always unexpected. I'd like to think of many things as if they're gold. Is there more to friendship other than becoming an awkward mall or public acquaintance? We go through phases and a lot of times we have interchangeable friends for those phases. It seems there are many things that are seasonal. I can think of people that I was close to in the past years and it becomes a Vh-1 special and it's like "where are they now?" where am I now? Maybe we'll say hello in passing and maybe we won't. Some people come and go like the wind and its like...thanks for passing through. I think about how terrible procrastination is and I feel bad for my share of it.

What's love really? We date people for many different reasons. We say that we're searching to find "the one," to keep from being lonely, to test someone out, or maybe even to kill time. And if that doesn't work out some people resort to fooling around, one night stands, and so forth. It's like when we go to Meijers...it's awesome to walk around and get the free samples but we never buy the product. Most girls go for wrong guys at some point in their life and guys go for the wrong girls as well. Dating bad boys, and bad girls, seems to be an epidemic.

If love only lasts for a certain amount of time...is it really love? It sometimes seems like its more of an infatuation than anything else and that's another Vh-1 special. We pledge allegiance to each other but it seems like in a lot of cases...it's only for the time being. Like it's a collectors item, limited time only. We'd all like to say that we still want to be friends with our former significant others but does that really happen? It's like once it's over, everything is over. If it's that temporary, then I don't want love and I don't want friendship. I'm looking for serious inquiries only. The butterfly "in love feeling," seems to be temporary and it seems like if someone is too good to be true...they probably are. If someone is good, it won't seem to be anything other than the truth.

Eleven Septembers

Everything is falling down on top of me
If only someone could help me, please
So I can see you and the way that you were before I left and
walked out the door
If I could promise something, I'd promise that I'll be home soon
I know I would make it if I could look in your eyes
So I go down on my knees, I'm to the ground now and I cry out
Can you help me? Someone help me please
Keep my love
Keep my letters
I promise that I'll be home soon
Leave a candle in the window
I promise that I'll be home soon
Erase the pain and make it right
I never wanted it to end up quite like this
I have my last letter wrote out and sealed with a kiss
If I could promise something, I'd promise I'll be home soon
I know I'd make it if I could look in your eyes
All this is burning, constantly burning
I feel pain in my eyes
Slowly dying, now I'm dying
I feel pain in my eyes
And to those of you who still fight for the cause...
The stone rolled away and left a stain
In my eyes, and in my heart
I'll give you everything that I am if you decide that I'm yours

Apartment Equals Party

I've got all this pressure coming from somewhere
Maybe it's time to deviate and unleash a scare
I'm somewhere between dependency and being on my own
I know exactly what I need and I'll get a room mate
So I won't feel alone
I'm getting an apartment
Somewhere I can be free
And keep my money spent
On one hand I'm still with mom and dad
And on the other I'm not quite adult
So if I make people mad or sad
It's my freedom and not my fault
I need to live and I need to feed
I'm through with slow motion
It's time for speed
Some may say that I'm under some influence
They may say that I follow, not lead
They are surely wrong because I have an apartment
I have somewhere to be free
I will go with whatever feels good
I will neglect things
That I never thought I could
I may leave things behind
Until one day I unwind
I will say that what I did was fate
Although I'm just starting to care
And it may be too late

I Kill Journals

We could always drive until the sun comes up
Something tells me that it's no more
Pick up the keys and the heart on my sleeve
They're abandoned to the floor
It's safe to say that you no longer dry my eyes
Not now and maybe never again
But there was this one time
Sometimes it seems this will never end
When the fire builds up I just walk it off
Although sometimes I just burst
Breathing in betrayal and exhaling retaliation
I murder every journal I write in
Whether it be good or bad
I show no mercy to the paper or the pen
Sometimes it's kind of healing
And sometimes it's an alternative to a friend
It's constant and consistent
In the battle of making things mend
Yes, I kill journals but it's not what it seems
I flood and release my emotions
And write down all my dreams
When you step back and look at life
We're all authors
We're just waiting to be seen

By The Wayside

Continue on, and I'll just lay here
While old thoughts just disappear
I was never one to look back
But it comes with the territory
Of leaving something behind
Compassion is turning around
It's something new
And it's not quite familiar
A burning question
And a humble heart
That time won't erase
Times of wellness never seemed to be
For such a figure
We're still sitting under
Our favorite tree, remember?
How it felt to be true and alive?
Wave good bye to the ships
As they leave the harbor
And fall behind the wayside
I couldn't have made
A more colorful diversion
There you are and somehow…
I'm still breathing
And my tears,
Are in excessive wonderment

Disclaim And Rename

Take me away with sweet ecstasy
Give me danger
Give me something new
I'll leave everything here
I'll run anywhere if I can run away with you
My every selfish desire becomes alive tonight
This is now and this is me
My target is plain in sight
If anyone gives me warning I will not heed
Because I've got what you want
And you've got what I need
I have the world at my finger tips
This person, this façade,
Is a drug I can't resist
Thank you for this high
It's created temporary bliss
This confrontation makes me mad
And makes me feel annoyed
As I disclaim all the things
That I truly have destroyed

I, Within Myself

I've got myself in a numb state
I've walked this far alone
I know I'm strong enough to keep walking
But part of me wants to hang my head
Part of me wants to lie in a lap and look up
Into beautiful eyes
The other half of me wants no one
Abandon all feelings of dependency
And leave them all on the open road
I've been failed, and I've been wounded
And I, within myself, won't die again
I contemplate what night has befallen upon me
That puts me in a state of pulling back
My outstretched hand
If the sky could cast a shadow,
My heart would lie in it
While my body ascends
And dries weeping eyes
On the clouds overhead
I will not collapse on anyone
I'm promised no tomorrow
And I'm promised no one
So here's to another night,
Where I rest my head upon myself

Confessions From The Balcony

It makes you wonder how far down
And if you've reached the highest point
I've never felt a breeze cross my face so hard
And you wonder if you'll fall into ashes
We're closing eyes and letting go
While the inevitable is holding on
This love is contaminated
I'm reliable in my attestation
And I'll always wonder
If love is a storm
And did I catch its eye?
All has departed
And there's nothing left inside
These feelings have many voices and words
But I hear nothing
I'm a little closer to the edge
Now we're getting some where
A sudden release and sidewalk graffiti
Then something pulls me and I return
To exactly where I came from
But I left a piece of me on that ledge
I don't have a physical depiction
But I did paint a picture
Of how it feels and how it can be
When it's just you and God
And confessions from the balcony

Relocation

It was like swallowing glass
From the moment your things left my finger tips
And fell to the bottom of the trash
I never made it worth throwing away
But it was time to relocate
I ran like it was a crime that I committed
I'm the only one who still remembers
It just doesn't feel the same
Putting my heart behind bars
To save what remains
But it's only because I have to
I never had an explanation
Just detachment and a one way ticket
That only led to no where
It's been so many months
Since you've seen my face
It's different now
And sometimes it still rains
I could count the ways that you'd say
"Depart from me"
Somehow that's not complimenting
It's been so many months
Since you've seen my face
But it was time to relocate
After you took me in vain

Handwriting

Seeing things torn is a hard pill to swallow
Every conclusion walks around in your head
And some things just happen
With no universal meaning or sentiments
Only to you, and the song you sing
Every hand writes differently
There's no telling what name I spelled
Or poison I drank
The glass wasn't filled with love
Just stage craft with elaborate sets
Wondering where it's gone
Yes, I do give kisses
Just not the ones blown in chalk
Complimenting the pavement
Stick figure tragedy
Dodging every tear, when they over flowed
Something had it bad for me
And I almost didn't get up
Just so you know
We don't always understand
The seriousness of "gone"
Or the seriousness of "sent away"
Every signature is unique
Time to find something else to spell
I don't know what poison I drank
But the glass wasn't filled with love
Stick figure tragedy
Just so you know

Parting Roses

Another pen in my hand
An ending to our story
Another nail in His hand
An ending to our story
Rise up
Rise up
The worst is over now
Good night and sleep tight
Remember we're alive
Forever seems so far away
A parting rose
Faith is the only way out
It's in a fighter's blood
To survive a broken heart
My love where have you gone?
You've been away for so long
Lord your love burns in me
Like a six shooter
Strait to the heart

Open Heart and Open Hand

Take a good look at this man
His open heart and his open hand
What about the way we said good bye?
His open heart and open eyes
There's no compassion for this man
Even with his open heart and hands
When someone says they love me
I don't take it very far
Could I turn the page and run away
Forgetting all these scars?
I could turn the page and make haste
So gently to your arms

The Tale of the Bump and Grind Chick

Once upon a time, I went to a Project 86 concert. The night was going to be filled with unexpected surprises and laughter. I was having an amazing time listening to the opening bands and an even better time listening to Project 86. That band has done more for me that anyone will ever know. I was standing up towards the very front minding my own business and enjoying the music. People started jumping around as a reaction to an amazing set. Project 86 has a street team known as "Team Black." Wearing hoods and bandannas, was the like an inside joke. All fans, and street team members, are supposed to wear this attire to stand out and draw attention. This was a genius plan to spread the word about their music. Somewhere in the middle of Project 86's set, I was under attack. I felt this chick dancing into me. The large volume of fans made it hard to turn around and see what was going on. This girl was practically molesting me from behind and started to bump and grind against me. I started to sidestep to get away from her but she followed me. I can't begin to express how violated I felt. As the congestion improved within the crowd, I was finally able to turn around and face my rapist. It just happened that she was a big Project 86 fan and was wearing the hood and bandanna. All I could see was her cat-like eyes. She wasn't too far from looking like a terrorist with the way she wore a hood and bandanna. I have no idea what made her do that. From now on, I'll be extra paranoid about wondering who's behind me. This concludes the story of "The Bump and Grind Chick.

Hope, Don't Die On Me Now

I don't know if I'm crazy for thinking this
Or if it's just not what I think it is
To day dream all day long
And compliment your forehead with a kiss
I don't want my hope to die
I threw my past in the trash
And I waved it good bye
Am I wrong for thinking and wanting to believe?
For wanting you to want me
And staying in an embrace
That I'll never want to leave?
I just don't know what to do
Maybe I should put my heart on lockdown
And keep all of this unsaid to you

Farewell the Burning Bridge

Farewell, the burning bridge
We pray soon to come
Farewell, the burning bridge
Farewell, the sky above
No, we won't take any more of your lies
In my stead, the truth was crucified
Bound and broken, I've been down before
I feel my life now
In this world of sorrow
You can never expect to feel better
Yet this is a mistake, you will be happy again

Down To the Very Last Thread

I don't know what direction the wind will take me in
Maybe back to when I had five senses and I was alive
I used to have a perspective and I knew what was real
I never knew it had to be so hard just to feel
A basic function that calls my name
And receives no reply
It had to be this way for someone like me
Broken down to the very last thread
To find a true self in someone else
The masks we wear are the barriers we share
With something a little less inviting
And reconstruction from within
Once I have forgiven I'll be forgotten
The right words escape me
I can't give something that I don't think I have
But the heart speaks on the mind's behalf
There's nothing left to say
We're walking remnants of modern tragedy
When you're heart aches
And your heart breaks
I used to have a perspective on what was real
That's distorted now and it's so much easier to self destruct
It never used to be this hard to pretend
One broken heart and bloody knuckles
It just takes time to mend
And it never used to be this hard just to feel
Broken down to the very last thread

We Need Human Rights Activists

I've heard too many vegans and vegetarians put down people who eat meat. Some of them get down right mean about it. They say it's wrong to eat animals and it's not fair to the animals. Animal rights activists say things like, "We give voice to the animals because they can't speak for themselves." Don't get me wrong, I think endangered animals need to be left alone and I think a lot of animals are cool and there are many I'd never dream of eating for food. So when someone tries to smother me about this subject, I always ask one simple question. Who stands up for humans in a shark attack? I'm not even kidding. Sharks take a bite out of humans all the time and nobody stands up to them for us. Maybe if we could teach a vegetarian shark how to speak English, and how to be an ambassador for humans, I don't doubt the possibilities. Look at what the sharks have done in some of the horror movies out there. Sharks eat humans in those movies and that's their main goal. They're not even nice about it. Sharks never ask if it's okay to do that. All those movies with shark attacks are planned the same way and I'm sure it applies to real life. Sharks aren't considerate, although, I wouldn't mind signing a peace treaty with them. I'm sure I could co-exist with them, even though they're not on my food chain. Maybe I'll stop eating animals when they stop eating us.

I Can Never Bleed Enough

The words I say have lost their touch
The things I left behind don't count for much
Someone tell me I've made it
And that I've opened my eyes
That I've stopped weeping blood
I can never bleed enough
I was confident that my heart
Was okay but the storms are setting in
I'm here tonight with an unwanted guest
In a time when I should be on my own
But stains don't wash out easy
There's nothing left to chase
Wave good bye to the coming tide
I was confident that my heart was okay
But the sun sets and the moon rise
I hide my eyes
Because my heart reminds of things passed
That I've stopped weeping blood
Because I can never bleed enough
I don't know what made me obsolete
But before you, there was everything

You Hurt My Head

Where do we reside?
I'll runaway on the midnight train
And surely hitch a ride
There's a lot of pain
Provided in cerebral display
All because you hurt my head and make me think things I don't
want to think
You make me dream things that I don't want to dream
Somehow you make me better
And that I don't want to believe
Why can't you see?
This should be you, being with me
The night is almost over and I won't feel the same
As I continue to go unnoticed
When there's so much to gain
I compare you to a rose
Because you can be so beautiful
Yet you only bring pain
I'm the greatest option
And you seem so blind
Tell me again
Where do we reside?
I'm not just tied to the tracks
But I'm under the train
You've been dedicated
To providing neural pain
All because you hurt my head
And make me think things I don't want to think
You make me dream things that I don't want to dream
Somehow you make me better
And that I don't want to believe
Why can't you see?
This should be you, being with me

How It Has To Be

I can tell by the lyrics of this song
That it's about us moving on
It's not right and it's not okay
But it had to be this way
It used to be the both of us
Now it's only me
It's not how I wanted it
But this is how it needs to be
I won't miss the heart you've broken
The one that you made bleed
The heart ache won't last forever
Because I'm recovering
Now the sky has such beauty
Because everything is how it needs to be
It really was forever when I walked out the door
Months of grieving and disbelieving
I finally can't do it anymore
I'm glad it happened I'm happy where I'm at
It took a long time but I finally realized
I never wanted to live like that
I will be loved

Dreamscapes

We lie awake with our blankets over our heads
It's time to sleep and time to dream
Forget everything that was said
Somehow our beds make us feel safe
Blankets don't just keep us warm
But they shield us from harm
Our pillows are a resting place
A place for our heads
Where the dreams are made
We hate the sun and its brightness
It takes us out of our escape
Waking up is the very last thing we want
Because the dream world is so much better than the real world
We have jobs to make us tired and to make us money
So that we can stay in our dreams
Dreams can be happy, sad, or scary
But we really don't care what they are
Because we take comfort knowing
That most of the time nightmares aren't true
And when the good dreams occur
We'd like to have every excuse
To believe they're real
So here's to another night of escaping

My Darker Side of Letting Go

Inject more anesthetic into my veins
It's the only thing that helps me over come
She has a way about her
A silent death and whisper
That only she can hear
She charms and enchants
But she means harm with every glance
She is the substitute for pain
And anesthetic is the analogy of faith
I am the conqueror with perseverance
I have no escape
Street lights and motor bikes
As the buildings scrape the sky
We're not one in the same
Because emancipating myself from her
Is freeing myself from the pain
I take comfort that love has been my weapon
And that I'm blameless
I did everything I could to resuscitate
But my hurt is long gone
No amends can be made to me
Because it's far to late
So I'll be quietly on my way
And you'll never be able to cast your shadow upon me
Never ever again
My once so called friend

Rooftop Release

There isn't a more beautiful view, than to see above man
I love the sky when you're so high up
There's no distraction from stoplights, people, and buildings
Sight is a pure blessing
Especially when you can see above the world for miles
And the stars seem closer than ever before
A table and a park bench are apart of the rooftop scenery
Weigh stations to stop by and refuel while you go on your way
Beauty can only be complimented by even more beauty
And when you're standing beside someone who has an abundance
of beauty,
The sky and cityscape look even better than before
So if nothing else, beauty is observed the best when you're
actually with beauty

You Broke My Home

I've heard it said that repetition with different expectations,
encourages insanity
Mom or dad, whatever the case may be, will make decisions that
will affect me
Whether it's now, or later, or when I have children of my own
Something may be carried with me to break my future home
Every solution is tried and the best that anyone can come up with
is acceptance
It wasn't my idea to be abused
Maybe not with their hands but with their words
Is my voice dead? Am I not heard?
I didn't know it was mandatory for me to accept something like this
Now I have a choice
I can have this end with me
Or I can put my children through the same
Some people never change and it's hard to know what to do
When you're around it all the time it becomes a learned habit
And it's almost impossible to stop
I don't know what to say or what to do
You broke my heart and you broke my home
I can't change you but I can change myself
And I'll never be alone

Ghost Dancer

I'm eradicating myself from the roots of this
Evil had to be purified by flame
They whispered outside my window
Ghost dancer, you'll never see my face again
You destroyed me and started off as a friend
I've collected your remnants in vials
And I broke them like glass
They're actors bleeding the part
Something doesn't look right
As I begin to clench my fists
I'm taunted by the words you said
The very thought of you is banished to sea
It was something I had to do to save myself
I raised my voice on everything that I saw
I runaway looking for a better day
And something new to draw
I have no conclusion to this shadowy fate
And now I know how it is
But it's too late
You'll always have a place in the fire
A demand and desire
Ghost dancer, you'll never see my face again
You destroyed me and started off as a friend
We'll always have Paris

Never Had a Pulse

I see the sun set in your eyes
There's no need to go anywhere
When the view is plain in sight
I once said that I feel nothing
Once you came across my path
I had to decide something better
I use to hide in the shade
By the hand of someone else
Holding ourselves in contempt
As a sound is never made
You make me feel complete
Captive by power lines
All the while and all the time
Your hand is a defibulator
When you touch me
My heart knows a steady beat
And my eyes are finally open
I just never had a pulse
I was filled with calibrated thoughts
There's no better analogy for freedom
Than walking around with broken chains
I've got prison break written in my veins
Somehow it's easier to breathe
But once I saw you I became different
You have the words that make a better me

Of Those I Do Not Speak Of

The dark ages have come upon me
A time period that I couldn't foresee
I had my one true love
There was no preparation to this execution
If I had been told the future ahead of time
I would have brushed it off like I'd been told a lie
The painted veil covered my eyes
I recited lines that I thought I knew so well
But the mistress of the pocket watch had a different story to tell
I guess it was time to change
Autumn leaves are falling and something is different
With style and endless drink
You replaced the void
And I became obsolete
The emptiness became your own
I did things out of desperation but it only hurt me more
Than I had ever been
Roadside silhouettes and graffiti goodbyes
Douse the fire
There's no trace of me
There are some words that we just don't say
And that's how I treat your name
If I'm ever going to be me
I'll never speak it again
And I have to treat all bad experiences that way

Hearts and Sandcastles

I don't seem to know what to think
Is the wind a sign of breathing?
Trying to continue what has been started
And I can't pretend I know the language
I fear the days
There may be nothing to say
And I've just prolonged my bleeding
My open arms and a place to stand
I can't help wanting to write our names into the sand
But I guess some pills are hard to swallow
Missing puzzle piece, nowhere to go
I lean on understanding until it gives in
Twenty-four hours needs to feel shorter
But time isn't something to kill
It's safe to say I just overdosed on my thinking
But I'm not scared and I don't care
Just as long as you ride shotgun with me

A Work Of Fire

Your eyes begin to glow
Just like embers that burn
I'm lost and I'm starting to gaze
I have no secret to hide
And I watch eternity pass by
It'd be worth any wait
To be by your side
I could cast a rose
Into a wishing well
A thousand times
But truth means facing myself
Honesty has no mercy
For someone who dreams like I do
I don't think you see the fireworks
I pray that you open your eyes
Because I still hope
I'm waiting for an excuse
To light the fuse
Set this potential on fire
My heart thirsts for more
Beyond the shadow of desire
There's so much to say
But I can't speak

Pave the Street

Sometimes I feel so invisible
And sometimes being steadfast
Means facing the edge of a cliff
There must be something missing
Maybe I should leave tonight
This very instance
Retreat to the shoreline
And disappear in the distance
As if thinking about love was enough
I'll be just fine
Even if it means falling on the finish line
Embrace the ends and cut my losses
Pave the street
Rebuild and take flight
Lock away my heart and restore me
I want it to be exactly how it seems
Everything I want
Remains an empty promise

My Pen Is a Blade

My pen is a blade
My paper is a wrist
I can express my pain in words
And give my heart a voice
This is the surrender of me
And this is how I bleed
When all is lost
When all is gone
I am the paper champion
And my heart is a notebook
This is the surrender of me
And this is how I bleed
I have had a harder life than most
I have had a better life than most
Life is the greatest trial of all
And when my heart is broken
This is the surrender of me
And this is how I bleed
I thank God that I'm alive

Letters from the Sky

Your love was the letters from the sky
And I won't be denied
You love was the anchor that kept me
From drifting away
When I'd gone astray
From the sky in fact
When I saw outside I looked up
I could I let it be something more?
How could I let it go?
Then I wandered so far away from you
How could I ask for your forgiveness?
I know now that I need God
I need Christ
I can take anything back
I will never go away and I will never feel the same
Inside of this landscape and poor reality
It seems I never learned to let go
I see inside my life so...
I never looked up to the sky
And I've always wondered why
When I can let it go
I can't face the fact that there's a debt to pay
And a price of blood
I looked up to the sky and you were always there for me
When I could care less about myself
You hold me and you lift me up
That I can lose myself inside of your beautiful eyes
Never have I felt the same way and now I share with you
You hold me in your arms and never let me go
I could never let go of things inside me
I could never cry
What I felt then, I feel now
I could make a way for you

My Path

It feels like I'm flying with broken wings
I feel the pain left in you
What I once said remains unspeakable
If you could make my heart unbreakable
It seems the word loved is being abused and misused
In the mourning each scar tells it's own story
It seems like we all get caught up in some kind of aftermath
Lead me on to my path
Lead me on to my path
When I reach the end and don't think that I will last
Oh God, light my path
When I'm blinded and caught in this world's wrath
Oh God, light my path
I lay broken but still my path is chosen
I've lost it all and I cry when stars fall
I feel the break and last breath
My heart aches and I wonder what's next
Take my hand and heal me, lead me on
To my path
God light my path
God light my path

The Folded Note

Sitting with the weight of the world on my thoughts
I didn't pick the seat that I'm sitting in
And I didn't chose the ride that I'm riding
I am kidnapped
I am the passenger
I know what love is and what it feels like
And I will kick, scream, and fight
Until I can fight no more
Every scar has a story attached to it
Not everyone gets the memo
I could never understand how someone can open
The door to your heart, drop a grenade in it
And expect you to stay silent
I should have hidden the key
I can't let you poor water on my canvas
My painting has beauty and you were in it
I've built up a tolerance for this change
But under no circumstances will I accept it
When an angel turns into beast, I cling to the angel
I am darkness
I am the sky
I know what love is and what it feels like
And I will kick, scream, and fight
Until I can fight no more
You're no longer the same you

I Am Many Things

I am a sticker on a spiral stair case
I am a signature on a bathroom wall
I am a picture in somebody's wallet
I am a picture in someone's hidden drawer
I am random objects that have reached a land fill somewhere
I am a 2:30AM insomniac that doesn't know when to sleep
I am a full length CD
I am a couple of EP's
I am a disc that is often put into my CD player
I am lyrics in a notebook
I am one greeted with hugs and handshakes
I am one that is passed by like I have no existence
I am somebody's joy, and somebody's regret
I am a hardcore fan
I am a fan of kung fu movies
I am one still grieving over deaths
I am still grieving, more importantly I'm still breathing
I can laugh to pass time
I can make others laugh to pass their time
I am still not very tired
I am an example of A.D.D.
I am an artist and a songwriter
I am a piano player
I am a steady wall in broken places
I am a cool dude
I am a ninja at heart
I am you

James vs. the Drug Addict

Tonight was like any other night. I was going to an electronics store to look for some CD's and to check out some martial arts films and then jump over to a clothing store that starts with a "K" to buy some awesome clothes. As I was leaving B.B., the craziest thing happened. I see this Caucasian lady, roughly in her 30's, being hand-cuffed towards the entrance. She was ranting, raving, and started throwing a fit as the officer took her outside. I finished my business and I was ready to leave B.B. I'm sure my thoughts about the incident were the same as any other bystander. I was wondering in the back of my mind..."What was that all about?"

I had a good idea of what happened when I walked outside. As I was walking out, I looked over and the lady was still shouting and four cops were yelling back at her. They told her to shut up and used some colorful language. Anyways, as I looked over, she pointed at me the best she could with her hand-cuffed hands and shouted, "That's him...that's the guy...he's got my money." I looked around and wondered if she was really referring to me. Sure enough, I was the only one outside and she was looking directly at me. At that point I was getting a little nervous that the cops were going to arrest me and I didn't want them to think I was an accomplice. The ghetto side of me was like "Oh no...I ain't got your money." Then she added something extremely off the wall and said..."Get him! That's the guy...he's got my money. He's the repair man that took my money!"

That's when I knew she must have been on drugs. I look like Chris Kattan, but I don't look like a repair man. The cops gave me a quick glance and then the four of them, at the same time, yelled "shut up!" I went on my merry little way. She caught me off guard and I was laughing my butt off. Then I drove over to the clothing store that starts with a "K" and a third cop car appeared at the scene of the crime. I don't know what the heck they were doing but I'm guessing the next stop was cell block six. About a week later, I found out that she was extremely strung out on drugs and tried to steal a large amount of candy bars. It's hard to believe that someone would go to an electronics store to steal candy bars. I guess if you do the crime...you do the time. Just remember to hide your drugs.

The Rider Comes At Night

To what end is my friend an enemy and an enemy my friend?
I sometimes comprehend the time when you just sat there gazing me.
The door was so elegantly open and it was time to leave.
What could have been is no consequence to what is, and can be.
It is now a red dead autumn because love just killed me.
Even though it was in my slow motion sleep...
I still dream.

Steve Rogers Is No Ordinary Man

It became so apparent that the end of something
Didn't have to result in a swift new beginning
Time was for the taking
Past loves dance with past regrets
Maybe I'm forgotten, maybe someday I'll forget
When all correspondence has failed and great words fall
meaninglessly to the floor
There must be some honor, some chivalry somewhere
Where every act is followed with great applause and the curtains
rise once more
I died a thousand times that day
When you became an acquaintance

Truth Be Told

With all that I have
I have never given you my all
I've had a song, and I've sang it for you
I just know it wasn't the best I could do
You're the bringer of wisdom and I'd never fit in your shoes...
To answer your knock, to walk in your foot prints,
Would be the best I've done and the best I could do
Even when my feet drag and my heart is severed
You're consistent today, tomorrow, and forever
My satellite, my refuge with love so great
The fire that burns, the breathe of life that dwells,
My rock...my faith...
You're the voice of thunder and the silent grace that makes my
words few...
To answer your knock, to walk in your foot prints,
Would be the best I've done and the best I could do

Story Book Love

Hand me a pen and I'll write us a better story
One where you'll slip and fall
For me, I request a moment time
Just a still life and frozen by your side
Let me paint you a better picture
One where the canvas conveys star lit eyes
Gazing, I request a moment in time
Just a photograph and framed by your side
Picture this, a memory...
In a place where hearts collide in
A collision, I say we'd be something to see
Just a screen play, handwritten by me
Hand me a pen and I'll write us a better story
One where you'll slip and fall for me

It's Okay

I've seen you do that sad walk
And the tears that hide behind your eyes
It just kills me every time
When I see that you're not alive
I can't scream loud enough for you
I never went anywhere
And you never had to cry
We could watch this feeling move
But we keep it in and go to a different room
Sometimes it's best to look unaffected
To become a clear vein where the virus
Hasn't been injected
I want you to know that this is a mistake you're making
And it's okay to fight if you're heart is breaking
So take a hand and make a stand
Hope is for the taking

Open Invitation

I've invited a pen to join my hand
As night time starts to begin once again
The moon is outside and neglected by my eyes
Because I know it's a wonder
And it's a surprise
My thoughts sing me to sleep
Not with unforgettable chorus
But unforgettable tragedy
I am my own enemy

Seas of Waverly

The waves of Waverly
I've fallen under your spell
And now I can tell I'm dying with you
You and I we danced together
But somehow we're lost
We lost ourselves
You and I we were so perfect
So young and so beautiful
Somehow when we began our quest
We went down with a misconception
Feeling cold and abandoned
As we struggle to find our hearts
And further rebuild our vessel
Upon solid foundations
We will drop anchor or set sail
As our troubled eyes seek greater horizons
Never again will we ever look back
Aching is the sound of our hearts
And the break inside our foundations

- Waverly Rd. is a street in Michigan that SakeRed got lost on for
two hours and I dedicated a song to it.

This Two-Step Is For You

Your savior awaits
At the door
It reminds me of a time
When I felt alive
And I could just go outside
And play my two-step song
Oh, the flame,
Reminds me when I felt alive
Resurrect the flame
And bring forth the ashes
Your savior awaits
At the door

Never Look Back

Will I be able to stay strong?
Even with my feelings gone?
Many will wonder how I survived
It's a wonder I'm still alive
Rather than become a part of the hive
It's a wonder I'm still alive
Now it's time to move
Move on
I will never look
Look back
These killing machines
Are killing inside of me
And I don't feel the pain of this anymore
This killing spree is killing inside of me
And I don't feel the pain of this anymore
Erase the pain and make it right
Now it's time to move
Move on

I am so awesome

I am so hot that when I walk past a fan it turns on to cool me
down with a gentle breeze.
I am so funny that clowns quit their jobs because of me.
I have the perfect height.
I am so awesome.
I am so cool, I pee ice cubes.
I am so cool, I glide when I walk.
Trust me...your mom is going to dig me and wonder why you
don't invite me over a little more often.
When I exhale, my breath is naturally minty fresh because I am so
awesome.
I'm so much fun to be around that I don't even go to the movies
anymore. People bring movies and pizza to my house so I don't
have to take my coolness out in public.
Every time I smile in the mirror...someone in the mirror smiles back.
If I wore a bucket on my head...it'd be the next trend because I'm
so awesome.
I'm so hot that those candies, covered by a candy shell, really
do melt in my hand, and they get broken down by anatomical
composition by the time they reach my mouth.
I'm so awesome; Santa sits on my lap and tells me what he wants
for Christmas.
I'm so awesome, there's always a red carpet in front of me to
walk on.
Anyone remember when Paris tried to copyright the phrase
"That's hot?" it's because she said it to me and wanted to make
money off of my awesomeness.
Then I pinch myself, and wake up.
Dreams are fun.

Revived and Restored

Tonight I broke the chains of torment
I raised my voice
Instead of making my thoughts few
And for a little while I remembered
But it was so nice to forget about you
I needed a change of pace
All is buried and gone
In the highlight of my face
Complete for a moment
Even just a little while
I was revived and restored
For once I gave a whole hearted smile
And after all the blood I spit
Months of tragic disposition
And one night of happiness is more than worth it
That's something I can honestly admit

Shoot To Kill

Before day breaks
There's a space in my heart
That's filled with those I can't save
God, give me strength
To watch them walk into a firing squad
And they don't see that there's another way
There's nothing I can do
But I can't pretend I don't see this
They have blindness
And a curiosity they can't resist
Delayed reaction turns into shame
I'll stand over the chalk outlines
There was bullet waiting with their name
I have to see this happen to you
There's room for my warning
And there's nothing I can do
I see the shifting shadows
I see what will happen
But you don't recognize the gallows
Whether I love you or not
This isn't the way things should be
You know it
But you still don't believe me
So God, give me strength
To watch them walk into a firing squad
And being left with the pain of knowing
That they can dodge the rain

This One Time I Punched My Cousin in My Sleep

Dreams are generally crazy. Sometimes they're serious and silly combined. Usually the things I dream are extremely weird. I once had a dream that all of my ex girlfriends were all best friends and loved to go shopping together. Even though it sounds funny...it really isn't. At some point, or another, I've had dreams where I've fallen off of something. Then when I hit the ground I would jerk awake. Then after that happened, it seemed like I had just landed from whatever I fell from. I once had a dream where I was thrown off of a bridge and when I hit the water I started to hold my breath. The crazy thing is that I was holding my breath in my sleep too and I woke up when I couldn't breathe any longer. This one time, I and my cousin, Scott, were sleeping in my parents' room while they were off on vacation. I must have thought I knew karate in this dream because I was being attacked by a swarm of bad guys that also knew karate. In my sleep I raised up above Scott and starting whaling on him. To me, I was still in dream world and somehow Scott was a bad guy. So I started punching him in the face without showing any mercy. He woke up immediately and said, "James! Why are you doing this to me?" By that time I was awake and I tried to smooth it over. I said, "Oh my God Scott I'm so sorry I don't know why I was doing that because I don't ever do things like that." Scott simply replied, "James, shut up and go back to sleep."

I Can Describe but I Can't Define

I can't put my heart into a paragraph or maybe I can
To say everything I have inside and convey exactly who I am
I can describe but I can't define
My hand moving the pencil in unison with my wayward eyes
It's not about what I don't have as much as it's what I want
I'm glad that what's left me has gone
And I'm thankful to God that I can look around me and see what's going on
I'm grateful I can use my tragedy
To counsel and consul others
And show them what happened to me
I've never enjoyed being so numb until now
The pain is quiet and it's easier to smile
But somehow it sometimes isn't very easy
I'm thankful that God could turn a lot of negatives into something positive
By going through experiences that my friends have gone through
Putting my hurt to good use is the least that I could do

You Should Have Stopped There

I'm worth a lot to my friends and to my family
It's my fault that I let someone determine my worth
Just because I'm worthless to one person, doesn't mean I really am
Anyone who only commits selfish acts, and spiteful acts, are not
credible sources
I mean something to the true people that truly care about me
I have a loving God that made me who I am and to him...I'm
worth everything
I can't allow one person's judgment to define my value
But love was involved
When you love someone, you take their opinions to heart.
And you almost believe them
The wicked are not the deciding factor for what stays and what goes.
I have to brush myself off and take a stand
There's nothing wrong with praying that someone should learn
their lesson
And we all know that there's nothing worse than getting a taste of
your own medicine
I suggest that you pick out the right prescription before you
swallow it

The TV Standard on Life

The media gives us so many perspectives and opinions. I have no idea what truth is when the TV turns on. Somehow right and wrong is easier to decide when it's off. I stay out of politics because it seems like what it boils down to is picking your favorite liar. It's so easy for people to judge our president but I never hear if they remember to pray for him. We've got to support him and our country somehow. Everyone is entitled to their own freedom and rights, but I have to believe that there's absolute truth somewhere.

Otherwise I'm just a lunatic that awaits padded walls. In my daily life I'm finding that there's a shortage of commitment. Marriage is almost completely erased because a lot of people settle for just living together and I can see the pros and cons even though I don't support that. Friendship seems like it's at an all time low. Some say it comes with getting older, but I think, in general, that many values are getting even more lost in the shuffle as time goes on.

Constructive Honesty

If I'm ever going to write the way that I want to, I can't always be apologetic about the things I write. It'll only hurt me in the end if I keep doing that. There's nothing wrong with apologies and there's nothing wrong with picking the write kind of words that won't hurt anyone else. If I'm ever going to be the writer that I picture in my head, I'm going to have to tread some water. There are too many instances in life that cause us to be cautious of what we say. I believe in God and I also believe that words can have a powerful effect on us and other people. Words have built me up and torn me in two. Words are even more powerful when used by someone we love or respect. I think we all cheat ourselves out of our own power of speaking. It's not just about saying something that could be taken well or offensively.

When you have something to say...say it. It seems to me that it hurts worse to regret not saying anything than to say something and regret it. I've learned to appreciate the simple things in life. For better or worse, I want to live. If my heart gets trampled on...so be it. All that matters is that I can get up once I've fallen. I no longer want to look through the microscope and see how I've postponed joy. How I've denied others the pleasure of who I am because I've got this mighty heart protected to the point where it's no longer visible. If I get hit...I'll hit back. I just hope it'll be constructively. If honesty is needed and it hurts you or someone else...then hurt.

Just remember you have a tongue. Stay honest and live like there's no tomorrow. Remember to speak, by any means necessary, and bring out the thunder.

Perils of the Canvas

Pictures don't need memories
Memories need pictures...
I have some glue and some scissors
Believe me when I say that I'm a master of my craft
Countless hours later and I have you
Full frame and right in front of me
If there was some sort of remote, I'd turn the subtitles on
And we could witness beauty in words
It's like saying the word "beautiful" for the first time and gathering
all of its meaning
I must admit that we were a vast painting with unlimited potential
Years have past now and so much is different
You and I are like the stars when day breaks
Then again, this is just a temporary breeze that I feel on random
nights
I don't think they make any pain killers for memories and I'm
pretty sure I can live with the subtlety of pictures
So hold on to your memories while you still can, because I'm
hiding the negatives

When Everything Is Gone

As I look back on my life today
Will things ever change, or will they stay the same?
I need a safe haven, and I need a shelter
God is my every thing when I falter
So when I sat down to write this letter, I thought of everything I
ever had to say
And I wrote it all in a paragraph that says goodbye
This is my last chance and I'll never surrender
A life consumed by pain, is a life that I remember
A new chapter about to begin
I thought you were my life, I thought you were my friend.
Now I know there's faith to believe
Ignite the fire that burns in me
No, I'll never look back and surrender
I am a casualty of this war
When everything is gone, you're all that I have to remember in my life
I'll never be the same
I am forever changed by the transformation that's inside of me
Even though I had nothing to believe
I know my life will never be the same

The Return

The return of your son
Forgive me, I've been gone
The return of your son
Forgive me, I've been gone
With a finale embrace
So content and so abrasive
Just one final embrace
So content, so abrasive
Rebuild my heart with my own hands
Though I was so far away,
You always saw your son
This is my return and I return to you
This is my return
My Jesus, I return to you
Rebuild my heart with my own hands

A Cloud

I feel that cloud of uncertainty hovering over me
Sometimes the mystery of tomorrow is the greatest gift, and strain
I don't really know if I'm walking a steady line
Or the trail to doomsday
I'm sometimes convinced that I will always be left having touched greatness
But never really experiencing it
When I fly, I silently expect to crash and burn in the event that if it were to happen...I wouldn't be shocked
I will have adapted.
Maybe someday I will be able to live and let go without the anticipation of crashing

A Drive through Drive By

What was...isn't
What is...will be
As wrong as summer, right as rain
The perfect picture is picture perfect
We all gallantly fall down under London bridges
April showers, may bring us flowers but July is the month that we will die for
This is my life now
It is what it is and where it's supposed to be
There's a lot of nothing to say
I have love as if I went to the store and bought it
I found it. I didn't ask for assistance, nor did I price check it
I found it. Scratch that...it found me
We have a shadowed forecast with slight chance of rain
Grab your umbrella because it will stain
So much at stake...
Did you know I dream in slow motion?
I do it because it posts pones the wake...
Thank you, dear Jesus, for the opportunity to be happy

A Knife and Something to Fall Back On

A knife, placed carefully behind me
So I'd always have something to fall back on
It's a type of poison that doesn't kill you
But makes you want more
All of them have forgotten about me
Tampering with evidence to expedite this request
Dirt on your hands that you'll never wash off
Whatever makes it easier to forget
She danced like she was intoxicated with love
With some sort of unknown composition
To compliment this window with my eyes piercing through
A bystander's shot at being symbolic
My face says it all in the language of despair
And my voice speaks in a manner of retaliation
 I'm against your gasoline intentions
A picture you burned to the ground
But I'll always have something to fall back on

A Note in the Shape of a Triangle

In this land of fallen timbers
I remember walking beside you
Your hand is cold and your eyes...like embers
As the emotions fly
Beauty falls
I expected a "hello"
But I got a "good bye"
Staring out on a day like this
I can't help but feel content
When you say you love me...
I hear, "I'll be leaving soon."
So let's remain silent if only for a moment
And pretend that this fire will consume
Staring outside on a day like this
I can't help but feel content

s.o.s. - sorry so sloppy

w.b.s. - write back soon

bff - best friends forever

xoxo - hugs and kisses

ttyl - talk to you later

t.a.d.m.m.h.f.b.-these abbreviations don't make my heart feel better

A Storm in Me Arises

Take my words
Take my life, and come back to me
There's a storm that arises in me
Hold me close, there's a storm
If I ever saved you from a knife
Then I am complete
I am complete
There's something I must say
Before we're torn away
Let's go back to the start of this
Before the wind set in
And betrayed us with a kiss
The day I died was the day I was reborn
I pray to my God that this chalice
Be taken from me and taken back
From where it came
Go back to whence you came

Your Everything, If I Could

I wanted to build you a house when it rained
And throw you a blanket when you were cold
I'd put your tears on my face so you wouldn't have to cry
I would place my jacket over a puddle so you wouldn't have to
walk around
I would be everything for you, if I could
If you were stranded on a mountain, I'd climb it to the top
And parachute off of it with you
If you're too tired to walk, I'll carry you
And watch you sleep
I don't mind watching, because I don't want to miss anything
Any opportunity to look at you, is more than an opportunity
As long as I'm beside you
There's no need to open the blinds, darling
You light up the room just by being in it
If you had a favorite song I'd sing it to you
Then I'd write one just for you
If you had any favorite memories,
I'd do whatever I could to bring them back, or reproduce them
One sundae two spoons
There are two open hands, because two hands are holding
But only until I hold the other one
If we could hold this pose forever
Our hands would never be empty

The Writer's Sketch

May I sit here and bleed awhile?
Perhaps I can hide how I feel and fake a smile
This distortion is murder
A front is all I have for her
In light of things unseen
My reality is so hard to believe
Who ever condoned the torture of me?
Somebody remove this veil
And allow me a brief moment
To unbury what I feel in an exhale
God help me to continue this fight
I can't bring life to these feelings tonight
Sometimes you have to come face to face with your hell
And sometimes all it takes is looking in the mirror
And identifying yourself

The Art of Taking a Break

I'm caught in between asleep and awake
But I can't sleep, and I can't wake
All I can do is watch my heart break
We're together, but we're not
Those were your words and they hurt a lot
You love me, you want me, and you don't
It's the curse that's left me glued to my phone
Maybe she'll call and maybe she'll leave me
My heart is weary as it fights this disease
Is there no end to pain, no remedy it can take?
It seems I'm left with time on my hands,
The art of taking a break

Pressing On To Overcome

I have been hurt
I have been toyed
Broken to say the least
At the very least I've been destroyed
A stole away traveling far
There's nothing left to say
We are where we are
There's a truth behind every selfish display
Acts of sin and changing like the wind
I'll press on with the greatest of faith
Through the mountains and over the sea
It's hard to take the hardest of heart break
It's a hard road to recovery
When I have been abandoned
When someone betrays me
But what's done is done
I will not falter
I will not run
It's time to finish the race
And pick up the pace
I'll smile once I have won

And I'll do it for myself

Sworn to Secrecy

Just like sand in the hour glass
Let's break the hour glass
Beauty was only seen by me
I don't think I know what it is
I don't think I can say anything
Without being killed by the everything
Because killing is what you do
And dying is what I am
There's a simple prayer to re-spawn from the ash
If only I knew what it was?
The words that I would speak
Lit gunpowder will fuse any wound
But the heart...that's a different story
As I pull away from one last addiction

Hey There Sunshine

Uprising and standing
The leaves are beautiful
Blood in the snow

Affected and Infected

I want you to have a little more than I can give
I want to be able to submit who I am, to you, without any doubts
Somehow I feel like I may be falling short of what you deserve
Maybe it's where I've been
And maybe my battle scars from long ago have shown themselves
Maybe there's no healing for this ailment
The one that keeps me from being everything to you
I have no bearings when I'm lost at sea
What anchors me to you?
After being ran over repeatedly I can't recognize truth
Its face has been so far from me
Its hand has dodged mine for the last time
When I'm affected and infected by the virus
The very thing that boils beneath my skin
So believe me when I say that you're truly amazing
And a shield like me has taken many swords
The road less traveled by paranoia
I just want to see you, and to see myself
See it for what it truly is and surrender
My heart is past growing weary
As it has entered into its reconstruction phase
It feels no pain and knows no worry
Even though I really do feel pain and I do know worry
It is the very essence of having a hard time
God please renew me
Complete me so that I can learn what it takes
To feel without fear
And to bask myself in her, who truly deserves all of me
To feel again without tainted emotions
But more importantly…to feel

Beauty is Pain

Call in case of emergency
Dial the numbers of escaping
All while the stitches hold true
In your head
And you think only you can make this end
You shot yourself in your imagination
The old you, needed a reckoning
And a wake up call from the police sirens
So far you're doing just great
You pick up the best selling book
The one in every lobby, prison cell, and hotel
With a few simple recitations
The old you is dead and gone
What remains is the graffiti stain
From the new ways that you've learned
The sharpest blade is known as a single word
To fall, to bandage, and cauterize one's self
After a stake through the heart
It can only be known as faith

White Lotus

The greatest find ordained in twilight
Amidst the fallen trees and snow
When holding onto the branches
And grasping for stability
Felt harder than letting go
I swallow words before I speak them
And exhale before response is given
Tragedy has nothing
With your arms wrapped around me
I see my reflection in your eyes
It seems what you saw me for
Lived just as easily as it died
One katana pulled after another
Your petals were soaked in ink
So your mark would never be
An unwanted souvenir forgotten by me
I can make a new life with new memories
Reevaluate the finger prints left in blood
What I have now is enough and it's everything
Pack your bags and hit the road
Amidst the fallen trees and snow
Feel your hands strain when holding on
White lotus, you no longer occupy this field

The Stuff That Makes You

I've always been told that if it wasn't for your past experiences, you wouldn't be who you are. All the good and bad things that happened have made an impact. This idea is meant in a positive way but that's not always the truth. Those experiences can keep you from enjoying the present if you let them. Some things don't die no matter how much you wish for it to happen. Some wounds feel fresh and though you live your life healed, you still bleed sometimes. Think back on the times that you've heard, "I love you" from people who thought they did. Think back on how you believed them, and they never really did. The sun goes down and turns your frown upside down. Times have truly changed. You read your own life like it's a book and you see how there was some good history and some horrible tragedy. You think of the friends you had but don't have. There's so much to miss, but the future is in the making. New happiness and struggles follow behind the future. I feel so symbolic tonight and I've drawn what I've seen in words. A toast to the old, and of the coming times, is in order. Drop your luggage and come out of it blessed.

I Put Some Thought into This

Maybe I don't have anesthetic but I remember
When I handed it off and passed it along
I walk through it like an alley and in a hooded sweatshirt
I parade around it taking the things I need
And leaving behind the things that I don't
I read this in a story book
One that I encircled before I picked it up
The best thing in my life only pulled me forward
While the worst pulled me to places I didn't need to go
Sometimes deathtraps wear halos
When I stumble and my hands tear into the sand
And my shoreline became farther away
When you're killed by things beyond understanding
It amounts to reprogramming yourself
I don't know where my father leads
But I will follow
Through sunshine and in shadow
To the edge of a cliff and by the wayside
While I pray that my dreams come true
Take my hand and lead me
When walking becomes the best that I can do

A Post-it Note to God

It's so hard to erase my hard drive
This anti-virus is missing your hand
I'm slowly losing you
Forgiveness is nameless
And I don't always recognize it
Leaving it alone is the best I can do
Seeking out a mending that may never be
It seems more worth it just to let it go
Pursuing that course corners me
Maybe you can forgive for me
Until I learn how
Sometimes the size of the crime
Determines its difficulty
But if you could after being killed
Who am I to say that I can't?
You're Jesus and I'm only James
I can't turn water into wine
All I can do is make ice water
Touching my clothes won't heal anyone
All they feel is the texture of the fabric
We both know it may not take all the pain away
So pull me up and onward
In the event that maybe I can be more like you

By Definition

My faith is strong
My walk staggers
Sometimes my hands are steady
And sometimes they shake
Now and again I say all the right things
But my words fall deaf to me when I say the wrong things
My bladed tongue
Was the very hammer that drove the nail
Somewhere over the course of time
I will break things
I'll make sure I don't break things that can't be fixed
And I'll buy glue just in case
I am where I am
I'm not my experiences
They affect, or infect, but they're not my definition
I am who I am because I always used a first aid kit
And kept my shoes tied

Flight through the Windshield

Never really knowing the luxury of being weightless
Everything that was said has broken down inside of me
I'm stuck between these things and the air gets harder to breathe
Sorting and sifting through remains but it's just not the same
I can't say that it was always this way
I speak of some kind of dream in a far and distant place
And I act like I used to be there when I never was
To become an escape two steps away and an hour late
Nobody really sleeps in a bed of roses
Loneliness wakes you into a sea of linen
And I was somewhere better a few minutes ago

You're Practically Invited

We were dressed in white and running towards each
The field became shorter as we advanced
Hand in hand
Stuck in a gaze that we become
The leaves fall and are ever-changing
A hopeful year lies ahead
It resembles a sign of clarity
No more reason to bleed
And avoid storms
When standing in front of a firing squad
It becomes less scary
Wake me up and let me know when you're around
Knock on the door and I'll throw you a blanket
Solitary confinement in my mind
I've stood my ground and I adore you
My fair maiden
Am I not at ease?
Hold me because I can stand
And become everything you want

Replace This Battery I Call My heart

It's the middle of the night and my voice is quiet
Nothing is heard and my pen drops from my hand
A distant view from the window
And a tear beads and streams until it drops
There was never any point in giving up
It was all just letting go
Crashing into the ocean and wondering where to land
While my grip is slipping out of your hand
Maybe it's my night to fall down
Replace this battery that I call my heart
And renew me
Speak your answer while I'm still breathing
Maybe it's not for me to dream
Nothing that I can touch but something I can see
When you listen you can't help but believe me
I'm so quiet and I hope that's okay
I'd say something
But I don't know what happened today
My silence is the confirmation
That the cliff wasn't as far as I thought
Replace this battery that I call my heart
Renew me
Speak your answer while I'm sleeping
I know you can see the tears I'm shedding
I'm ready for what you'll say

Elusive

I was all that you wanted?
You transformed like a car wreck
As if a locomotive could speak
False words that spoke to me
Let's not and say we did
When I ran away, I lied awake at night
Dawn came too soon
I saw it all frame by frame
For a thousand years to come
And you stayed elusive
To everything that you did and said
Ride until tomorrow
When night starts to fall
I'm not sure what happens when I back out
Stay a distant memory

Incite Your Weapon of Choice

Hold your breath and take a dive
Become the mainstream quota
When ink outlines your hands
I'm not affected by the sky
So say exactly what's on my mind
Walk beside me
Check your wrist
You know exactly what time it is
Opposition, my love
Recite the words
I love you
Even when your seasons change
These retaliations lay heavy on my heart
I let you go and fell to the floor
Let me know what it is you see
What you devour and what you believe
Hands held and reaching forward
Shoot a flare and I'll find you

Shimmering Lights and a Nighttime Scene

Fear and I, struck up a conversation
I was afraid that there was too much to say
It weaves my heartstrings against the grain
I wrote it down for no one to read
But I want you to see
You can't be lonely when you're painting a picture
All the beautiful colors that take place
And I've got us in the spotlight
Believe in me when you don't believe in anything
Shimmering lights and a nighttime scene
Your pulse is evident in the way you move
The words that can be said
Watch closely and I'll show you
The shades of my eyes and what they say
They're starlit when they're dripping blue
When two hearts take concussive pictures
They lose their translation
My eyes widen and sleep sound
While my heart waits for you
Come around and I swear we'll make it out

Take Your Drink

Maybe I'm an alien with nowhere to go
Glasses empty and drinks seem to flow
I have no place here because I don't conform
There doesn't seem to be anything but this idol
It's staring me right in the eyes but it's nothing I can swallow
Maybe you can hold that much
And maybe you're just hollow
An emptiness that gets filled
When your thirst betrays you
And your body falls to the floor
You get carried out
When all the while I'm nonexistent to you
Because I do not swallow what you swallow
I don't impair myself with a false repair
Some hold it well and succeed but there's no guarantee
That you'll wake up tomorrow in a better state
Perhaps now you will see
I shouldn't be pushed away
Just because I don't drink
At least not as much as you

The War Inside of Me

Why can't a fairy tale end well?
Instead of a horror story
You can hear me say, Oh Lord
I want to be less of what I am
And more of what you are
I can safely say that your hand
Is the only hand that keeps me from the flame
And pulls me from the water I'm drowning in
I want to read a chapter where the wind is at my back
And pages that scroll in clarity
When I fall, don't give up on me
I don't know what happens
When I turn around and run away
Times of joy and sorrow
My own shadow lurks an uncertainty
The alley lights say, "I'll make a man out of you"
I can't be too far down, I still laugh
The inner fears that implode
I can't be too far gone, the end is still untold
Love has taken up too much space
But there's always room for it
Room to make me and break me
The hidden and visible ailments
The rise and fall that you'll see
You can hear me say, Oh Lord
I'm a man who breaks shackles
And fights the war inside of me

Asherly and a Sign of Faith

My last birthday was the worst birthday of my entire life. I was hurt and broken hearted and it was the one year anniversary of my grandpa's death. I faked every single emotion I had that night. I played a show with a side band that I was doing for fun. It was my birthday wish to play a show on my birthday. Giving specific details might be a little too damaging of me but I will say that I had been extremely hurt by someone. I was walking around the venue mingling with friends and people I hadn't seen for a long time. There was actually a birthday cake at the venue waiting for me and this show was out of my town. I was tore up bad and God worked some magic to get me through and to show me he was thinking about me. So here I am...a hollow shell of a man. I was walking around with fake smiles and laughs and then it happened. I was walking by and I felt a hand grab my arm. It was a girl named Ashley that I had met through my favorite venue and through being in SakeRed. I can't remember exactly what she said when she grabbed my arm but she said something like, "Are you okay?" It was like hindsight, she knew I was hurt.

I hadn't talked to her enough for her to know what happened to me at that point in my life. She pulled me outside of the show and talked to me. She listened, hugged me, and prayed for me. She even got misty eyed with me. I silently asked God for help that entire night. I kept repeating the same phrase over and over in my head. "Please let something good happen tonight..." That was one way that God acknowledged that He was thinking about me and that He wasn't going to let me hurt alone. I just wanted a miracle no matter how big or small it might be. I didn't care. I will never be able to explain how she knew I needed help or that my heart was broken. More broken, than it had ever been. In our greatest tragedies, never underestimate God. Never believe for a second, that He doesn't care. This was just one sign out of many...that I was not alone. He used Ashley to relay the message that He was going to lift me high and out of the snares I was in. I couldn't begin to express just how grateful I am for what she did. To some people it's nothing more than talk therapy but it was more. It was the simple fact that I needed to be prayed for more than anything and it happened. I admire her for giving me the time, and for being such a good woman of God. It's a prime example of how we all should be for others in their time of need. I'm thankful for my friends for doing their best to make my birthday special. Thank-you, Ashley.

Resurface to the Deepest Ocean

I was pretty sure that I had drained the poison from my blood
But every now and again, you'll get an onset
Hang your head because another time goes by
It haunts you and you ask yourself
Was I alive back then?
I know I existed but so much has changed
Since then I've become more than I could imagine
Sometimes it's so weird to be yourself
Looking back on the times of hurting
Not everyone will own the things that they do
Would you turn on the safety?
If you knew the damage a bullet can do
Once you've fired
Run away from disinfecting because it hurts more that way
What was it like looking the victim in the eye?
When the knife was turned and said you loved me once
Not only is betrayal exactly what it's defined as
But it's also honesty
The foretelling of another when you feel time is through
We all consist of layers some
And some of the dark surfaces resurface into the deepest ocean

Evil Defined

The door closes and locks
Now it's time to put on the cape and cowl
You're on your feet, costume and all
Giving in to every evil deed
We think these things are okay
Because we leave them unseen
Tonight like every night
It's in you and it's in me
The things we do that are not ourselves
And against what we believe
It goes on for a long time
Until you pull yourself out or God makes it cease
Evil: our greatest disease and exile
He sees behind a closed door
He sees your deleted internet files

The Wounds Were Visible

I started to disbelieve
When there became less of me
It hurt no matter how it seemed
I thought you'd know
All I had were wounds to show
I may have left but you let me go

I wasn't sure how this could be
But the events that were left unseen
Had never included me
The unfolded empty notes
Meant the stories became untold
The moment you let me go

It wasn't clear from what I had seen
Maybe I was a want and not a need
There was never a fight for me
The choice was made, the words were **bold**
And winter never felt so cold
I had to leave because you'd let me go

Bed and Breakfast

I asked you to come inside and you did
You were cold so I built you a fire
You needed conversation so I kept you company
When it rained I gave you an umbrella
When you were wet I gave you a blanket
You were too tired to go home so I kept you for the night
You couldn't sleep so I told you a story
I kept you warm, I kept you dry, I gave you a story, I kept you
safe, I kept you company, and I kept you embraced

On another night I asked you to come inside and you said no
I offered you a fire, a blanket, an umbrella, a place to stay, and a story
You declined every offer and said you didn't want to be near
You said you had somewhere so much better to go
And I asked what better place than here?
You packed your bags and I waved good bye
You didn't look back and I wondered why
I was sad that you killed my hospitality
After I did my very best
Even though I was just a path behind you, I couldn't stay sad
Because it wasn't long until I had a better guest

My Heart and My Hand

Please God, tell me I'll be able to fly
I wasn't a good son to you before
But I'll repay any price
I want blessings and not trials in disguise
I've never expected to be stable for long
It's not so easy to recover
Some stitches keep falling apart
I don't expect more than what I deserve
But God, she may have my heart
Broken watches make it hard to tell time
I'd take it all back for being so blind
Maybe you can forgive me and make this one good
I'd burn down my walls and I know I could
My crimes have all been confessed
Just tell me this is the answer
And that this will make me blessed
I'm afraid I won't have and lose again
I would deny my own heart
But God, she holds my hand
And I don't want her to let go

The Hero's Shade

There are some puzzles that are hard to solve
When you face your own
It takes away from dispositions
A man must face alone
When stepping forward means getting pushed back
Still reaching for the stars for a guided hand
Exhaling water and with no bandages
These are his vices in which he will stand
When he speaks alone he's speaking for his self
When he speaks alone he's speaking up for himself
Stuck between a rock and a hard place
It's in his endurance
He becomes afraid
Any place he can lay his head
He will call home
But it's so much easier said than done
He reads a book of many authors
Hoping the answers will search for him
Looking for the perfect words
That will be rehearsed
To take the clutch from his darkness
And shift into reverse
I become afraid in my endurance
Now the man is gone
And the warrior remains

Mending the Outcomes

I don't care how this could be
Just as long as you're next to me
These outcomes seem alone
The world's shame
Came along when it forgot your name
And I can't say I feel
I still bleed and I'm not free
I just want you next to me
It's everything that I believe
It gets harder to stand
But the nails weren't in my hands
You take away the things I feel

Drawn In

Would I give in?
And be drawn in by familiarity?
Pulled limb to limb by fabricated memories
Yea, well, those memories are dead
I can't pretend that nothing was ever said
A Passerby on a subway station
Sits alone and now he's gone
And the people carelessly walk past
I've never seen a pedestrian quite like you
In and out of another's life
Just to see a plot thicken
And keeping another's dream from coming true
It's beyond me, why I'd want to be the old me
I had never been blind until the moment I met you
I don't know why I'm being haunted
But once I see my blessings, this quickly fades

Tale of the Haunted Pants

I've come to the conclusion that my pants are haunted. Last weekend a can of pop exploded in my pants and yesterday....they mysteriously fell down while I was burning some trash because that's what I and my family of hillbillies do. I would have burned my pants to drive away the evil spirits but I desperately need pants. It'd be different if it was just one pair that was haunted. I can't spend the rest of my life wearing shorts or in my underwear. I don't want to live the rest of my life in fear. I must battle these entities. When the pop exploded, I kept wearing them and even contemplated pouring the rest on myself to finish what was started since half of it was gone. If it was my shirt....it'd be more understandable but why my pants? What could be so great about them? (Other than they're cool and I wear them) either my pants just possess evil or there's some perverted ghost running around that likes to disrupt my dignity. Cool ghosts don't rob people of their pants. Now that this is happening I can remember back to a much earlier incident......

There was a time when the entity possessed someone and her friend to bully me to the ground and take my pants. I know that sounds bad but had they not been possessed...they never would have defeated me so easily. I was caught off guard until the spell cast upon the thieves broke and my pants were returned. By the way, girls can't beat me up. I'm tough. I'm not sure what caused the entity to resurface but I'll be looking further into the issue. The only explanation that I can come up with is that this entity was sent from the dark lord of the abyss and lately I've caught onto the pattern. It only happens on weekends....

Let me assure you that there's nothing funny about this. I'm just a nice guy fighting to keep his pants.

The Scene is Dead, Long Live the Scene

I'm not sure how this came to be
Every town is different and varies
And some places have an amazing scene
I just have to speak out on the issues I've witnessed
And the things that have affected me
Constant trends and values fading away
Fashion rules in a place that had values
When the music stands against a crowd of crossed arms
These common places seem to be consumed by staring faces
And messages are rarely heard
I feel out of place in comparison but I belong here
Sometimes I see favoritism and popularity
The very places I went for escaping
Became places for defacing
The feeling of unity and uprising
Feels few and far between
There's only one thing that keeps this running for me
The familiar people that'd still die for their beliefs
I came to be a brother and a friend
Not a temporary solution to a temporary trend
Time is passing
Scream, chant, and dance your heart away
That's what it'll take to revive the movement of this place
Cover the wick of a flame burning fast
I am no one's outcast
Your scene is dead
And mine...very much alive

The Midnight Train

Rain against the shoreline
The tides carry me away
The sand grazes my skin
And silence breaks a heart
The tides carry me and fade me away
It's the first time since then
And I knew you wouldn't know me
Pass me by and continue your course
Wayward directions and I stand still
I don't know if you ever healed
Because I don't think you were ever hurt
Your capability determines your senses
And I stare up to a stormy sky
Before lightening strikes my enlightenment
It felt so good to leave the stockades
When the power had no longer taken me over
Freedom and emancipation
Catch the midnight train with me

The Struggle behind our Eyes

Sorrow hid behind your smile
Suffering a loss triggers denial
Into the void of despair
We all share a common pain
And fall short of becoming one with ourselves
Whether we're destroyed or exploited
The farther and farther we search
We're afraid we won't find the answers
We embrace the fight
We embrace the endeavor
To live free today, tomorrow and forever

Remember, a Rope Can be a Good Sword

The scenery that turns our heads
And breaks down our doors
Bound us together and tied us to endless floors
Travel on oh gracious host of night
A fire burning in my heart as my ghost takes flight
Of you, I always demand and pay the price
To take back my hand above others
Or break like swift innocence my brothers
Today is the day of our greatest triumph
Preserve what's inside and let go
Stay who you are and become a better version
Never forget your name and never forget your home

The Forever Fall

Forever is inside of a heaven that is one less breath away
For you, I'd wait an eternity
But I remember how the knife seems to turn in me
If your memory was a pill I'd swallow you inside
I may not be able to walk a mile in your foot steps
But I can follow behind
You're so much more than what I am
When you take your eyes off of God
There's no limit to how far you can fall
Let's just pray that we're on the right course
It's so easy for it to go unnoticed

Lost Flowers

You began to move and speak differently
No news is bad news
The hardest choice was what poison to use
Cast as a thorn in your side
You weren't the gift I opened
There's nothing wrong with my eyes
But I should have worn glasses
The blinders seemed so transparent
I eventually caught on but it was too late
There's nothing to show for this
I can't believe that was more important
Than my smiling face
I became a welcome mat at your doorstep
Because of what I am, I finished last
The words fell to your feet
And I allowed myself to fall into defeat
Relearning how to stand
Over how broken I am
Nothing could be farther from the truth
It seems this fresh bouquet has nowhere to go
I'll wipe my face and say, "never again"

One Man Army

Nothing is impossible
When a cause is involved
A gift of thrown over tables
To those self appointed
Consider the scales tipped over
An action taken
When a page can't be turned
Nothing comes that easy
Beliefs are hard to maintain
Adversity has no face
I'll get back on my soapbox
I can't be permanently thrown off of it
The batteries for my megaphone will never die
My mic cable will never be cut
This will breathe until my voice shakes and my heart gives out
I won't let anything wash my brain
I won't forget the promise
The day we are silent about what matters most
Is the day we die inside and turn into a ghost
An anthem is better than a gun
Save yourself if you can...

Drink Deep

A model citizen so complacent
There's no such thing as a heart replacement
I ran to you because I recognize refuge
The dawning age is coming
All the dots are connected
I guess my mood never stabilized
And you can't blame me
For not whispering back to the shadows
Man made it
It never made the man
Wellness became a formal party
All dressed up and no place to go
But I'm holding up a sign
Clarity, don't forget me at the gates
Drink deep, I need you full and not empty
Clarity, don't forget me
Soon we will rest

A Better Place

She said, "Pray for me, I believe God hears you"
I must not have prayed enough because she died
I questioned if God could really hear me
My pleas must not have been recognized
This feeling didn't last because I know there are different paths
A better place awaited her and I can't feel guilty
The human in me wonders if my prayers could've saved her
Death is forever defeated and I remembered those words
They're not the words of a false prophet
But the words of a nailed promise
And I remember the sound of His voice

There's always a Soundtrack to Heart Break

The date and time can be quoted like a recitation
We remember exactly where we were
We remember what songs played in the background
And what songs soothe
Venom in the veins
It's all like a parasitic nature
Therapy is a reminder of pain
And after we listen
Some songs will never be played again
Go back in time to better days when a song didn't torment
Translate the sound coming from the speaker
Breathing life into the story
Soon forgotten
There's music for every occasion
It begins to remind me of life incidents
Road trips through the snow
Into the grasp of anguish
In the absence of words
Music carries the conversation
Suddenly it becomes your voice
And I never had the chance
To appreciate the music for what it was
It became a killer in composition
And pieced together bad experiences
The good experiences have no songs to damage
Break the cd, break the radio, and switch the tapes
I can silently slip into escape
I can write my own music
So what can I say?
My works save me from the soundtrack of heart break

The Empire Falls

It's written in the shadows
Because there are some things
That will never be known
Some secrets that will never be told
When you believe a lie
It's written on your heart
You'll know that it's perfect
When it's fully believed
And it's so plain to see
Your empire falls
She'll hold my hand and watch it with me
I sold myself for a lost cause
To become something unfamiliar
The farthest version of myself
But my former life has passed
The comfort in seeing something end
Is being able to say it's over
It's not enough to set our senses on fire
By the damage that's fluently speaking
The walls continuously closing in
And the air circulation that was cut off
My former self has passed
And so has the poison
Your empire falls
And she will hold my hand

Notable Injuries

For a while I will be transparent
The lines are so carefully drawn
When it strikes midnight
I'll have a name and I'll have a face
If I don't make it back, send forth a search party
I'm more exclusive than previously mentioned
No different than the sound of rain on a tin roof
Speak easy, time is short
Tearing at the seems on a quilted pattern
I can remember what it was like
And it was never quite like this
We're carried along
But nothing seems to phase our addictions
It seems we're all on strings
Survival depends on breaking
The last link in the chain
I remember thinking there was nothing taller
Than all the things I looked up to
It's the narrow scope of things
That sees us just how we are
While we wait to be revealed our destiny
We sustain notable injuries

Do Not Tear Holes in My Sails

I'm not worried about what's behind me. I only care about what's in front of me. I have eyes on the back of my head so that what's behind me…will never sneak in front of me. Needless to say I carry my luggage. I just make sure my luggage never carries me.

Life isn't any different than bare-knuckle boxing. If I told you that my lip had never been busted, I'd be a liar. I guess I think it's more important to live through the fight than to admit defeat or worry about winning. If you live through it, then you win because you weren't stopped. If you break your knuckles in the process then you've earned your right to a bonus round. That means you simply kept on fighting.

My words, and my attitude, can really affect your happiness. I can make things harder for you or I can make them easier. Making life harder for you will only make it harder for me. I just have to choose to see it that way. I can be the cause of a fight, I can endure a fight, or maybe I could stop a fight. I can feel like a ten car highway wreck and still make your day better and I think that's the way I want to be.

Documentary of a Dream

Inject me with all the words I've needed to hear
Never mind the blood
It just means the truth is near
We share a common vacancy but that's no remedy
That's just the chance we take
Digital escape plans are made
By the hands of the sleepless
And in the hearts of the restless
We now see what we want to see
We live how we want to live
Finally, we film a documentary of a dream
Utopia in the making
Flawless and absent of mistakes
Troubles and sadness
It's a false reality that we believe in
Harmless lies that we tell ourselves
Daytime recesses in aged film
They either take off or stay still
Eternal desires we want and need
An executed action when there's nothing to say
Our lifelong goals that we want so deeply
Hanging on us like a wraith
So I'll forever dream in slow motion
Because it postpones the wake

Brotherhood

Interlocking shoulders, friends and brothers in arms
There's a lack of attendance so sound the alarm
Whatever happened to, "I've got your back?"
My brother's battle is my battle
My brother's pain is my pain
No wound to be made and no wounds to sustain
We were one but now we're two
Nothing stops the noise we make
Until someone falls out and falls away
A battle of subtraction
Our unit dwindled to every man for himself
It could be that we're getting older
Or times are truly changing
We were many but now we're few
Pledging short term allegiance to each other
Out of everyone that I know
Only a few will stay and they'll be the words
They'll be truth
They'll die for a friend
Eye for an eye and tooth for a tooth
What ever happened to the loyalty of a friend?
Or brotherhood that knows no ends?
When my legs fail me I question who will draw the line
Or who may drag me to finish the race
Search your heart and question what it's all about
Who has your back without the shadow of a doubt?
Make a pact and swear an oath
It's all we've got in this world

Wilted Petals: What Happened to You?

Once you were a great flower
Now a mere reflection of a former self
And beauty withheld
You ran out of sun and water
Your heart gives out
What happened to you?
With a shrug of the shoulders you're gone
I've lost contact with the ground
And your signal is slowly fading
Your amazing coat was shed for the rags of confusion
We were once skyscrapers
But now we're privately owned buildings
Waiting for the opportunity of vacancy
Your struggles are infinite dimensions long and wide
And a mile deep
You lose sleep and don't even know that you are
Life is in order or so it seems
With or without me
Roots that grew into the foundation
Have pushed away the loose brick
Mindless drones that have no home
All the times that you thought I didn't care
I never left out my concerns
And I never let your fines go over due
So this is me, asking a burning question
What happened to you that made things this way?
What happened to you?

A Night with You

I can't shape the way I feel
Or sculpt the calmness that becomes me
I'll treasure you deeply and pull you closer
The only blade that doesn't cut
I watch you with your eyes closed
I'll take your hand and make the simple things proposed
Sign a waiver or contract that says that you're real
Say that you don't just visit in my dreams
But that you stay awhile
I'd share the city skylines with you to see your smile
Tell me stories that end the way I want them to
Hard medicine to swallow when the trees tear the clouds
My shadows fall into place when you walk closer
My words are full and meaningful
The greatest adversity has nothing on you and me
Come this way when you're scared
And when the nighttime makes no sense

Bad Medicines

It makes a person wonder
If he's swallowed poison his whole life
With a shimmering glimpse of terror
It makes one wonder if he can hold his own
There's nothing stable in instability
Just mobility and hoping
One day this will be better
If now's not the time...maybe later
It's a shame to wait for the train to go by
And settle for eternal sleep
That's what you get
When you feel your wellness is out of reach
I don't know if it's a test of faith
Or if it's a man-made threat
This is something I take every night
Pray for the best and lay to waste
Until the road is uncovered
And the chariots can move
I've never seen a body so weak
When the spirit is always willing
Our heads pound in thunderous rhythms
We make way for deadly interventions
They won't soon follow because everything is wrong
With a shimmering glimpse of terror
I wonder if I can hold my own

I Need Truth Instead of a World without It

Repetition Is in my blood
And I'll be whatever they say I'll be
I'll do whatever they say I'll do
The statistics are small for breaking the cycle
But that's so far from the truth
I consist of bricks and adhesives
No uniqueness to say the least
Predestined to be what's come before me
But that's so far from the truth
It's not over until it's over
They say I drift from one direction to the next
But I follow my own path
I march to the beat of my heart
And create things that never existed until I came to be
I'm not a can of soup
I'm not generic
I am my own name brand without a label
I've heard that I'm a continuance of a never ending assembly line
Predefined and suited for a crime
Found in a dictionary and declassified information
But that's so far from the truth
I stare oblivion in the face and show no mercy
And I become invisible
When all is decided and I'm at the end of my rope
They say destiny doesn't wait for me
Even after I change my stars

Sights to the North Star

Some things expire
It's time to write something new
Why I'd look back is beyond me
Some grasps are hard to escape
I'd step into snares but I watch where I'm going
When I feel that hand, I'll set it on fire and press on
I'm headed somewhere so much better
I never had to settle for "broken"
When I could write something new
Follow the sun
There are some arms that are so much better to fall into
Your pocket is full of broken glass
And you act like there's nothing wrong with sharing the wealth
Oh God, keep my sights on the North Star
Set my eyes to my blessings and not another's curse
Most spells don't last long and when I breathe the midnight air
I'll let my lungs expand
Knowing that truth fills them
I'll recognize the reflection I see when I'm standing over a puddle
I'll know that it's my own
And my heart will beat in sequence with your words

Words to the Apathetic

Some think there's no reason to care
As far as they're concerned
Our souls don't go anywhere
Keep writing with a broken pencil
Using lead that won't erase
Destroying everything in your path
Leaving no room for remorse
It won't purge all your mistakes
Yet you damage, run, and hide
In a nomadic kind of state
Voiceless to an extent, we raise our hands
Are we all living like eternity can wait?
Oh, no…no…no
Because eternity could be on the brink of today

Be My Beautiful

The most colorful shades seem to take me over
I could lose myself in the depth
I'm suddenly reminded of a sunset and a stormy night
The beauty of clouds and lightening
Much like an answer and hindsight
A compliment to the canvas
I'm thankful for the dreams that replace the fallen ones
Losing something is the same as dying
But to have a better replacement
Now that makes me speechless
I'm not afraid anymore
Whether it be over a cliff or down in a valley
Falling is perfectly fine with me
Just as long as my hand touches yours
There's no plummet involved
No death to be welcomed
Just the voice of beauty
As mystical as the falling snow
Be my beautiful
The answer to an unanswered prayer

Say this isn't Me

When your head is just above water
It makes you wonder what joy can be tasted
And what dreams can be lived
When things pull you under and air runs out
I don't know if I should involve myself in what makes me happy
If it costs my life and I can barely stand
The point of origin can't be traced
The performer is dead but knows the show must go on
Receives no enjoyment from the things he loves
Lifelessly carried from the stage with no contrast or color
I need a different camera because this isn't how I pictured myself
I believe in endurance and recovery
A shell of a former occupant walking a tight rope
Scarred beyond recognition
Just say this isn't me

Next in Line

It seems the past has more than one face
Using photo albums to reference the applicant's experience
A never ending process I thought redemption could erase
Excessive baggage never lets you walk alone
Next in line for the vaccination
They never come for free
But truth serum is on sale today
I get pulled away and led by the hand
When the skeletons open the closet door
They don't always belong to me
But I've seen them all before
Your cover has been blown
And your contact has been made
You've set up a monthly quota
But forgiveness takes it away
Consider the bomb defused

You'll Never See

You could be blind in both eyes
I think you underestimate how much it hurts
To constantly be reminded of who was the popular choice
In that instant I have no voice
Talking wouldn't do any good
It's a lost cause and dropping it is the best
I just pretend that you silently care about me
That you saw my good points and that they count for something
It's made a hard condition to work under
And still I'm not at rest
Because I know things should have ended differently
You don't think so
But then again I am where I should really be
As far as you're concerned, I just never measured up
I can't tell you what's wrong because you won't see it my way
You'll have reactions that will only make it worse
I was a better guardian than I'll ever get credit for
With me, there was never anything that you had to worry about
But it's always about what I consider treasure
I'm not a pirate but I kept my valuables close to my heart
All I'll ever get is the slam of a judge's hammer
There will never be resolution
I'll never understand your reasoning
And you'll never understand that I loved your loved one
I can't say you ever suggested fixing the leak in the roof
Or to rebuild a bridge that was so carelessly broken
I may not be your favorite but if you'll open your eyes you'll see
The best loyalty and chivalry came from me
Your faithful friend
I am where I am for a reason

Black Listed

My views are distorted
It makes me push everyone away
Because everyone is capable of the unimaginable
It may only be shocking to me
After you're around someone for a while
You take them in and take them for their word
For quite some time I picture everyone with daggers
Hid behind their back looking to compliment someone else's
I still find myself looking at everyone that way
In the wake of the disaster
I became a monster
Someone I no longer could recognize
The deepest and darkest betrayal
I'm forever changed by it
And that part of me will never be the same
I have you to thank for it
Apologies will never fill the void
Will never be accepted
And will never repay
In my heart and mind
You are dead to me
I had a funeral for whatever I thought things were
I sometimes think I'm evil for this area
But it's not a sin to cut off
To disconnect and disinfect
Anything less will hurt me
My heart was visible and taken away
An open wound that cold hard steel replaced
I guess I've blacklisted more than I thought I'd ever have to
Forever filtered
And it breaks my heart

Dynamite in the Vacuum Cleaner

A new part on the assembly line gets no name
Gathering up information to support the claims
They say it is what it is
There's no hope for you
Coming from a world that talks in circles
To distort the truth
The product of experimentation
Always subject to change
The end result determined from an environment
These changed file types don't feel the same
When people we love become people we don't know
And they don't even change their name
So many are lighting off dynamite and having a blast
I guess the world can be a vacuum cleaner
Sucking in the people we know and the people we don't
The corporate response is that it was an accident

Final Dance

Frame by frame you're digitally frozen
In the back of my mind
And in an editing room
Constant loops and feeds
The light is flashing and you're on
It's your time to fly
To see through someone else's eyes
This is how I pictured things
And I can't compromise myself
This conversation is so abrasive
I never knew things were this empty
Fill yourself and make yourself visible
In the world of imposters and false impressions
It's the queue for the final dance
The music doesn't have to change
I don't want this to end
Tell me I'm not the only one who sees this
Disguises can fall to the bottom
Of the cutting room floor
I can't begin to convey the weight on my mind
This conversation is so abrasive
And I can't compromise myself

Speak Easy

I've given up on heart conditions
And meeting the requirements that follow
I refuse to take the offer
Of all the things that trail behind
It can be so disorienting
If you have a lot on your mind
Excavating brand new ruins
So metaphorical for myself
I close the door just for a second
As this persona starts to escape
I resurrect fallen honor
Because I found something I can keep
Life is breathing into my ambitions
A sunshine that will be eternal
With all the colors of expectations
I finish out my words
It's not something I want to carry
But it explains who I am
My eyes say everything you need to know
When my lips fail to speak
They're no different than a book
Something you have to know how to read
They say everything
So speak easy

A Haunted Day at the Haunted Cave

I think it's crazy that people pay to have someone else scare them. I'm talking about all the fun-houses that everyone goes to during Halloween. There's a haunted castle, cave, forest, jail, and an Egyptian tomb where a pharaoh gets his revenge. It costs nearly the same as going to the zoo except when you go to the zoo; you're not expecting to get scared unless a kangaroo punches you in the face or something. People will wait in line for hours, just so someone else can scare them. Just walk down any alley in the city and I'm sure you can get scared for free. These haunted places remind us of the places, and things, that we see in the movies. Maybe that's why we're so addicted to going to these haunted places during October. A lot of girls are easily spooked and guys only go so they can protect their women when they jump in fright. Guys love to watch their girlfriends scream and get spooked. Then again, I also think that guys go so they can have an excuse to go down a bunch of slides. It's a haunted place…not a playground. I have to admit that it really is fun to go down the slides.

I also receive a lot of enjoyment watching the employees dress up and scare the girls that are waiting in line. Girls get so zapped into their conversations that they don't see these spooks sneak up on them. The spooks aren't the only ones who have fun though. I'm good at sneaking up on girls too. I sneak up behind them and get my face so close to them that it almost touches their face and then they jump and scream. One thing that I have noticed is that when you scare someone…there's a split second where their brain connects on what they're seeing and they smile for a brief second before everything really starts to click. Then it turns into a jump and a scream. It is so much more fun to be apart of the scaring than just watching it happen.

There are signs posted everywhere instructing the customers not to touch the workers because allegedly, the workers won't touch the customers. Sometimes reacting to these moments of fright involves some kind of touching. If you get the living day lights scared out of you, it's not unusual to do something back out of reflex. I remember when I witnessed a worker going irate to a police officer accusing this woman of touching him. He got right up in this poor women's face and she just jumped due to him scaring the heck out of her. The guy yanked his mask off and ran over to the cop saying something like, "She touched me! She can't do that. I'm a worker." Then he looked at the woman and said something like, "You touched me! You can't do that!" If I had a brick, I would have thrown it at him just to get him to shut up. It was just a reflex accident and he was acting like psycho.

Naturally, I can't go to these places without experiencing something extremely strange. Weird and crazy things happen to me all the time. I was headed towards a "porta-potty" to use the restroom and my first crazy incident of the night was getting ready to happen. I turned the handle and proceeded to go in and I heard a freaky voice say, "Hey!" It was really dark but I could see a hand reaching for the door with lightening quickness and I freaked. No one ever leaves the door open on one of those things. They're usually in the dark somewhere near a park or festival. I envisioned this forty-five year old truck driver sitting in there doing business. I also pictured him coming out and seeing me waiting to go next. At that point I was pretty sure that he was going to walk out and snap my neck. I didn't care at the time really. My mentality was, "If he's going to kill me, I hope he at least lets me use the bathroom first."

I saw the door handle turn and out came this huge burly, body-builder looking man. Except the street lights revealed this sasquatch to be a cute girl around the age of twenty-one and she was very short. She squeezed past me and giggled real flakey like and said something like, "Hee hee…oops. Excuse me." I scratched my head in bewilderment. I could not begin to understand how this happened. I heard the voice of a lumbar jack come out of that porta-potty and out comes this cute little girl. It was obvious that she didn't have a sex change or a manly voice when she came out. I guess the embarrassment of being walked-in on scared her and caused her voice to bellow through the trees. None the less…I was scared. Then I finally got to do what I had waited to do for an hour or two.

Naturally, something else crazy happened when I walked out. I was walking trying to catch up to my group and low and behold...I tripped on a power cable for the Haunted Cave. I saw some of the food stands go black, among other things. I heard this old lady's voice yell something like, "Larry, one of those dumb kids tripped on the power cable again...go check it out!" I did what any other citizen would do in that situation. I ran.

Can you tell me How to Get to Club Neptune?

My first and only car wreck was like a huge circus. It was a very rare night and many events happened that normally don't take place during a car wreck. I'll proceed with my interesting story. I was on my way home from watching an Easter program at a church and I'd say it was around 12:30am. I was driving around a round-a-bout and some idiot turned one-way on the round-a-bout and hit me head on around the corner. There was no time to maneuver or escape. I didn't even see the guy until he hit me. My beautiful car had the front pushed in about 3-feet from the tank he was driving. The only damage he sustained was a broken headlight. That wasn't fair. They both got out and acted as if they had just got done smoking pot. I was mad because he clearly didn't read any of the signs. A cop showed up and filled out a police report. He ruled a "no fault," because the other guys said that the sign wasn't clearly marked. The sign was a little crooked and was slightly faded…but it was visible. The cop knew it wasn't my fault but decided I would be the first to get a breathalyzer test. He barely questioned them at all. He interrogated me like we were in the Vietnam War. He said something like, "Son…have you been drinking or did you just wake up?" I told him that I don't drink and that I didn't just wake up. He said, "What are you doing out so late…are you sure you're not on any drugs?" I told him that I was going home and that I had just got done watching a reenactment of the last supper for an Easter church service. He looked at me like I was lying.

I grabbed him by his jacket and I said, "Listen here bucko. These dummies turned on a one way road and hit me head on." Okay, so maybe I didn't really say that but I guarantee that I was thinking it. Then something completely random happened. This guy in a white Jeep pulls up and talks to the perpetrator that hit me and says, "Hey…you made my sandwich at Subway earlier!" The perpetrator replied, "Yea bro…that was me." Then the guy in the white Jeep said, "Okay, see ya later." This was totally random and nuts. What are the chances of anyone stopping just to tell someone something like that? I think the chances are slim. A fire truck and an EMS pulled up and just start talking to one another. After a half an hour the driver for the EMS walked up to the cop and said, "Well if you don't need us for anything we'll go ahead and take off...thanks!" It was almost 3am and it still wasn't quite over. I was waiting for my brother to show up and take me home so I could escape this mess. I became very depressed about my car being totaled and depressed about how the night had turned out to be one big circus. Then the most unthinkable thing happened. Two BMW's pulled into the carwash, right next to the scene of the accident, and they rolled down their windows and called for me.

There was one Caucasian female in a car full of gangster looking guys. She had a very weird voice and began to talk to me. She said, "Hay! Can you tell us how to get to Club Neptune?" I walked over and politely told her I didn't. She mentioned all these roads by it and asked if they ring any bells. I was so furious about how the night turned out and I decided to be a total jerk to her. I kept telling her that I knew of the club but didn't know where it was at. She began to hit her hands together and repeated, "Do you know how to get to Club Neptune?" I replied, "No miss. I can't tell you. All I know is that you can go down Coliseum Blvd. to get in the right direction. I've had a long night and I need to go now." As I started to walk away I heard her annoying voice repeat, "Hay! Can you tell us how to get to Club Neptune?" I walked back and said, "Look lady...I have no idea." Then she said the most ridiculous thing to me. She said, "Hay! Is it okay if we follow you there?" I couldn't believe it. My totaled car was the only one left from the wreck and I was the only one around so she had to have seen how messed up my car was. She seemed completely oblivious to that fact.

I couldn't stand it anymore. I was getting so sick of her asking me the same things and not respecting my privacy over the whole situation. I won't lie...I replied with some colorful language. I cussed up a storm that could have watered a crop for a week but I'm not going to repeat any of it. I'll just give a generalized summary of what I said and I felt bad enough for using that language. I said something like, "Lady looked at my busted car. There's no way in heck that I'm going to take you anywhere!" She rolled up the window and said, "Fine then. Forget you!" I was so happy to hear that and I was happy to see them leave. I received pure joy because I didn't have to hear her say that menacing phrase anymore. So never ever come up to me and say, "Hay! Can you tell me how to get to Club Neptune?" If you do…I'll rip off your arm.

The Ending

So I guess this is it
My final stand against the grain
I want to say I did some damage
That I fought it all with my words
Perhaps the beast inside of me will be gone
I hope I killed it
The only way to be sure is to keep moving forward
Take it out of the basement and into the open
I've made my faith visible and my heart ache felt
Because we have to be human together
One day, the thoughts and memories will be gone
A former life has passed and now there's new air to breathe
Cleansed beyond comprehension
My new wings unfold and the pain is gone
I recognize what I see in the mirror
I fell and got back up
I left and I returned
Maybe I'll finally be able to sleep
And rest a lifetime away
As long as I'm waking up in your arms
A breath of life and fire into my words
Embrace me and never let go
The war inside of me is at its end
I've fought for so long
Purified and purged through words
The glass I've carried no longer cuts
A message I'll be sending
And a time of closure
As I've reached the ending
I've never felt so alive

Cardiac Arrest

Every time I watch myself bleed
I know it's because I missed the card up the sleeve
This virus makes its way up to my heart
And dances around in my mind
I've long since been a punching bag
My losses are apparent
But it's clear to see that I'm clearly yours
When a shadow comes over me
It makes me hold your hand tighter
I don't want it to kill me just because I'm scared
It speaks for that time period but not for my silhouette
I only want to pull you closer when the tides rush in
I don't remember being under cardiac arrest
The seasons change when you're policed by your own heart
But I can't give up and let myself down tonight
There's still so much to conquer
The owner of two shaky hands
Who has just been handed his life
I have a fighting chance to get it back
I can't let myself down and I can't cut myself short
When I occupy this corner and feel the threat
I reach to you like you're the only one who can get me out
Remember me when the candle is blown out
I don't want it to kill me just because I'm scared
With your hand present
I can't cut myself short

Means of Transportation

To live a life without the right name or face
Is to surrender true identity for sake of the norm
There was a lot of hostility when I arrived here
I couldn't take a plane instead of a bus
I had to take whatever was available
Yet there was such prejudice against how I got here
I went through the duration of my stay
Never knowing how you felt before I got here
A lot of minds changed
All it took was living for awhile
Your darkness would've never been known if I wasn't told
But there's nothing like hearing the details
I guess a blessing can arise from wrong doings
I'd love it if that were me
Sometimes I toss and turn in a dreamless sleep
Knowing the ones I love felt that way
And I never had a choice on what avenue to use to get where I am
I've strictly done everything I could possibly do
I couldn't let these bags get heavier
But I look to the sky because I know how to be
How to raise my hands in the rain
And wash my hands because I had no choice
I changed minds by being alive
But had the right mindsets been applied...
There'd be nothing to change
Lying in a dormant coma and breathing with hesitancy
I have immunity knowing that not everyone was like this
I have my own purpose and when I look to the sky...
I realize none of that really matters anymore
Then I wake up completely refreshed

Talk Therapy

Sometimes I speak my mind too often
I try to bash the injustices with my vocal chords
I thought I kept talking about the past
To show how the present is so much better
Somewhere along the way, I got a little carried away and blind
It wasn't quite talk-therapy but I thought it was
My constant reminders weren't decreasing the pain
They were hurting you
Someone I care about
Someone so true
I allowed the venom to stay in my blood too long
Now look what I've done
I pulled down the shades on the sun
Washing my hands didn't get rid of all the dirt
I got mixed up in myself and caused you to hurt
You should know what I see when I look at you
Now I can go outside and play in the rain
I stood on my feet because of you
I smile wider and breathe without hesitation
There's more than I've said but I can't tell you
Maybe one day
I'm brave enough to say that I don't know what I'm doing
But I do know what I want and who
The day gets better and shines brighter
Who I want is none other than you

Thou Shall Not Kill Merry Christmas for One Nation under God

There's a sad argument that goes on every year when it hits the month of December. There are many people in the United States that want to abolish Christmas. Every year I turn the T.V. on and watch these outspoken advocates. We could go over a long list of reasons to abolish Christmas but that's not my side of the fence. It's a shame that some corporate businesses change their holiday displays and even tell their cashiers to say, "Happy Holidays" instead of wishing them a merry Christmas. Sometimes these businesses don't even want their employees to say anything all together because they may offend customers. I don't think that's fair to the employees that want to express those things. I personally wouldn't be offended to be wished well from a person of any faith or belief. The overall goal of these holiday wishes is to look at your fellow man and wish them well.

I can't believe how many people out there cringe when they hear the name "Christ" added to something. I give props to the privately owned businesses that won't change their holiday beliefs just because a few people don't like them. There are a lot of people who celebrate Christmas whether they're Christian or not. This subject is always so controversial to some people. So there's no need to make an argument about a celebration. I guarantee that the majority of those people, who oppose Christmas, won't complain about getting a day off of work. Some people go the full mile to put a damper on a celebration that a mass majority celebrates. To this day, the most sincere "Merry Christmas" wish I received was from a Chinese man who was clearly Buddhist along with the rest of the restaurant staff. He even bowed, which is his country's way of shaking hands. I returned the respect by saying thank you and bowing back. I'm not used to bowing to someone instead of shaking hands but I did it anyway. It wasn't a big deal and sharing respect is more important than the minor details. That's how these occasions should be handled, instead of running to the courthouse like a cry baby.

Somehow posting the Ten Commandments in a courthouse can offend some people. I guess separation of Church and State is taken very strictly. Some of the murderers out there need to be reminded that killing someone is a bad thing to do. Even if I was an atheist, I can't say I'd argue about posting some good universal values in a room that is constantly occupied by criminals, lawbreakers, and liars. Then again, who am I to say we should? All of this adds to the list of silly things that a minority of Americans want to take away. I guess it's just exercising the freedom to do so but I think a workout on a treadmill is more beneficial. The pledge of allegiance is gone, and next is the national anthem if it isn't already gone. I think it all boils down to being a respect issue and respect isn't a law. It shouldn't have to be one. Hopefully we adult enough work things out rather than abolish any of traditions we have whether it be publicly displayed or not.

Conflict Revolution

I'm collected in vials
Extracting all the things I need
Show me an open wound and we'll stitch it away
There's no reassurance on what becomes me today
I believe the accepted term is, "down"
Give me a method for pain and then send me on my way
Walking the city streets until I find someone like me
After spinning in circles for so long it's hard to know which way to turn
Breaking even and making it out alive is all that really matters
But it never hurts to get a step ahead
I have something to tell you but I don't know when it'll be said
My heart's involved and that makes it harder to go in, all or nothing
There's got to be some instructions for reconstruction
It seems a bit too far away
Those three words were always said prior to the execution
You can only die inside so many times
Then it's time to fold and pack up the cards
Pack up the scars
Move to a new location
I want to turn myself in to you
And become paralyzed in your custody

Crazy Daze

After some of the crazy days I've had...I get reminded of how precious life is and how lucky we are to be alive. How we want people to love us, and that we want to love them back, because love really is amazing. We've all be dealt bad hands but there's a blessing hiding somewhere. I think of the times when I've felt alone and didn't remember that God made everything and is in everything. The only thing that's alone is our human emotions. Things happen for a reason. Some things in life really suck and you just want to punch a hole in the wall. In my book there's nothing wrong with that. While I'm punching the wall, I also want to see the big picture. How God will turn a bad thing into something really good. I don't have any issues with apologizing for things that I should apologize for. The phrase "I'm sorry," is just two words. It's the lack of those two words that can cause so much turmoil as well as the lack of sincerity when they're being said.

Stole Away

Set the stage it's time to go
It's out of character for the time being
Letting out the spores of change
You were a water fall
But you've been a dry river all along
You used to stand but now you lean
Past phases don't do very much
I watched you walk away
It was clear you were done with your work
Setting out early for quite some time
Your rose follows you as a reminder of beauty
I'd hate to see you get hurt
Advances and taking advantages
Look at what you've left behind
I tried reaching out many times before
It did nothing none the less
And I thought it could work
The parts were missing and the mechanic took off
I could have been your friend
I watch you sink and I watch you plunge
Nothing I said took away any weight
You're even more distant and I'm accustomed to it
The fates were chosen by you
You'd use any excuse to ship up and ship out
It was so long ago that it didn't even happen
And it doesn't bother me anymore
But every once in awhile I almost remember

I See So Much More

The future story isn't clear
What lies ahead is an identity unknown
I'd love for it to be the things I dream about
The one I'm always thinking of
I can't think of tomorrow when it isn't promised
Hope can be so complimenting
I just hope it's where I'm headed
Because I've hidden myself for far too long
I didn't come all this way to leave empty handed
She's there in my dreams
Shadowing over and singing me to sleep
When I wake I want to see the sun rise
Knowing that I can touch it and that it's within reach
Never in my life have I felt calmness
In the wake of a casualty
It's no wonder I'm fear stricken
Strait through me and to the bone
I'd walk down a side walk all night to get a glimpse of you
With all the sights, my eyes turn into cross hairs
And I know what I'm looking at
I'm seeing something to work towards
And something to hope for
If I'm dead wrong I'll become blank
And a refugee back in hiding until the sun is out
I could never convey exactly what I'm thinking
The fear of loss is too much to bear

At the End of the Tunnel

I see growing petals that wind around me
You've got a kiss and I'll lean in
Forever seems a life time away but I don't mind waiting
Tell me the station is at the end of the tunnel
And fear never resides there
I've never been promised anything
Maybe you could put one together for me and say it's you
I'd love nothing more than to rest my head on your shoulder
And watch my feet sway
I'm lifted by total emotion and I think you can tell
I've kept a secret and a mystery
Thoughts of you are like music
Soothing melody that's looking for me
Leaving ruins behind me as I'm guided
I have a hand that's pulling me forward
That's where I need to be
As long as you stay steady
There's no reason I can't tell you
Accomplishing things that I never thought possible
I'm drowning and you saved me
From everything that cuts
There's no reason to feel otherwise
Just say the story ends with you

I'm Sorry it's Missing

I lost something that I can't get back
Final notices sent and it's too late
It was something I might want you to have
Giving away to the hands of the dead
A part of me is in shade
But no part of me belongs there
I'm so sorry but please accept what I have
A shooting star on the right path
There's always the deepest chamber of my heart
That's never been fully occupied
I let it go
I've let you down but you're not the only one
I'm walking a fine line and I'm empty handed
Until you grab it and claim it as yours
I wish I could give more but I can only give what I have
Tell me a story without an ending
And a journey that will forever last
My steps are quiet
I abandoned my post and we can see where I am
I'm forever in debt that you opened the door for me
And left a key under the door mat
I can't say there's anywhere else I'd rather be
Than completely and totally
Next to you

A Few Things That I've Learned

I've learned the power of desperation. I've learned that it's easy to be taken advantage of when you're in that state of mind. Desperation will make you say and do crazy things if you let it.

Never date a band roadie. IT NEVER WORKS.

I've learned that friends are amazing. I've learned that many of them are only amazing to your face. They can be very deceiving and that can work against you because they know you confide in them. Although, one good friend is a million times better than any amount of bad ones. Those kinds of friends are few and far between, but they're truly amazing.

I've learned that love is insane. You can use it to change people, places, and things. It can very well change you too.

I've learned that people, in general, are selfish. We all have a dormant evil inside of us that only focuses on ourselves from time to time.

I've learned that being a vocalist in a hardcore band means you have to look a certain way to be believable. My spiky hair dew, preppy tee-shirts, and skater shoes, don't send out the vibe that I am a vocalist with a mighty roar. I used to feel like people looked at me as if I were a stand up comedian, but they were soon convinced otherwise once they saw me rocking out.

I've learned that gas station sandwiches aren't always the best to eat on the way to a show. I will admit that there are times when they really don't taste all that bad. This falls under the commentary mentioned above. The commentary I mentioned above pertaining to desperation.

Never talk about how much you hate your software vendor at work. You never know when they might be on speaker phone for a conference call.

Time Capsules and Bombs

I am convinced that a part of us says, "It should have gone
another way"
Wishing life, death, happiness, and bad fortune all at the same
time
My grudge is your grudge but I've held it much longer than you
have and I'm not letting it go as it will surely do me in
I hate you; I forgive you and all at the same time
You destroyed the best thing I've ever had and created something
better
Time is the greatest test for friendship
Sooner or later I'll find out who is truth
To some friendship is a trend, and fashionable
They pick their favorites and ask the second best to die
Since we simply don't have the time...
I will, however, cherish you for the time that you are true
And for the time that you lied to me
In day to day life I see walking remnants and walking ghosts
You just may be my time capsule and I'm willing to keep you
buried
Past + present = instability
And I can't let go if I carry things with me
So good night, sleep tight, and let the bed bugs bite...

Torn Away

I'll spare the details and the long story
I can't say it happened to us but I can say that it happened to me
Humbly loving someone and stripped of all dignity
I saw the rose but never the thorns
My hand bled so much while I was trying to hold on
There was no doubt in anyone's mind of who I was
And my adoration
I became a different person that day
And I wasn't me anymore
I was a shadow of my former self
There were many different things that I suffered from
My lesson was well learned
I give you all the credit
So many different questions
It made me wonder what kind of man I am
It made me wonder who I really knew
I pray that you find your way
But I also pray for lessons to be learned
Until then, we will never be able to relate
I had to depart everything from me
It was the only way to get the poison out of my veins
I threw it all where it belongs and it hurt
But I had to find solace and I had to do it for myself
God knows the truth
I'm writing this to say that I'm finally me again
There's no question that I had my devotions
If I can help it, I'll stay the missing person on the milk carton
To all the things I shouldn't be
Solace will happen
I have faith and that's good enough for me

There's a Better Way to do this

Don't throw in the towel, just fight fair
Because just below the hands…
The lines are clearly made
I know what you're trying to say
And I hear you
It doesn't have to go this way
There's no need to make this a final solution
Just voice your concerns
And no letter will have to be written
No scene will be found
The team will have one more player
To get into the game
I can't say I blame you
But it's not what everyone wants
I'm pretty sure you know what book gives the answers
And if you open your mind
You'll see whose arms you can fall into
I've got your back

The Weight a Burden Can Weigh

I don't know when the eye of the storm will be reached
I am just a man
Fleeting to safety and away from harm
It's not mine to carry forever
Wrongs to right and compensate
Repaying with the shake of a hand
Wandering to the end of the world to throw it away
But it's not so easy to land this plane
My footsteps become deeper and the weight breaks my shoulders
There's no other means of escaping
It's time to confess and break the hour glass
To cut down on the time to walk so far
They say it can be done but it doesn't feel like it can sometimes
Submitting a work that's not clearly seen
And haunting in my dreams
I can't let the terror outweigh my responsibilities
Falling on the floor and onto my knees
I've got some things to admit
And do the time for all the crimes
I don't know when the eye of the storm will be reached
I am just a man who no longer needs to carry a burden
Farther than it needs to go

The Walk that Never Dies

My inspirations are all that I have
At the end of the day I cling to an ideal
And that can never be killed
I may never shake your hand
Or meet you face to face
But I'd give you a bandage
No matter how far away
I'm cleansed and purified and my ailments are gone
I gave my heart and soul to make you smile
To make you feel better
I pray my mission is accomplished
My ship may have holes in it
But I still set sail
The tides will turn and I'll never go down without a fight
I pray my words find you
And speak to you if I can't be present
This is what I made it to be
An avenue to the fallen
Another heart to read and share
I did my very best to finish what I started
I don't know what lies ahead
But there's nothing that these ideals can't change
Rest assure I'll still move
As long as the war inside me rages
I'll die to get that bandage to you
I may stumble until I drop
But I'll keep walking by your side
And that will never stop

Printed in the United States
100121LV00002B/337-348/A